An Alphabet of Authors

Robin Works Davis

Fort Atkinson, Wisconsin

Published by Alleyside Press, an imprint of Highsmith Press LLC
Highsmith Press
W5527 Highway 106
P.O. Box 800
Fort Atkinson, Wisconsin 53538-0800
1-800-558-2110

Cover design: Frank Neu

The paper used in this publication meets the minimum requirements of American National Standard for Information Science — Permanence of Paper for Printed Library Material. ANSI/NISO Z39.48-1992.

Library of Congress Cataloging in Publication
Davis, Robin Works,
An alphabet of authors / Robin Works Davis.
p. cm.
A companion volume to An alphabet of books.
Includes bibliographical references.
ISBN 0-917846-62-1 (alk. paper)
1. Language arts (Early childhood)–United States. 2. Early childhood education–Activity programs–United States. 3. Reading (Early childhood)–United States. 4. Children–United States–Books and reading. I. Title.
LB1139.5.L35D39 1996
370.6–dc20 95-43053

Contents

Introduction

An Alphabet of Authors brings together young children and quality literature. It offers ideas for sharing this literature to librarians, teachers, parents, or other adults who work with children in preschool and the lower elementary grades. The purpose of this book, which was written as a companion volume to *An Alphabet of Books*, is to expose children to a variety of authors and a variety of different styles of telling and illustrating stories.

An Alphabet of Authors is arranged alphabetically by author. Authors included are new and popular, or more prolific authors whose books are considered classics. Many multicultural authors and titles are also included. Books listed are generally award winners or recommended books that are in print or commonly available in school or public libraries. Review sources for titles include *Children's Literature Review* (Gale Research, 1976–1996), *The Children's Catalog* (H.W. Wilson, 1996), *School Library Journal*, and *A to Zoo: Subject Access to Children's Picture Books* (Carolyn W. and John A. Lima, Bowker, 1993).

Each letter of the alphabet marks a section that includes information about the author or the author's books; thematic ideas using the books; an annotated bibliography of books to share; chants, action rhymes, or songs; activities; and an annotated bibliography of additional selected books by the author. Activities are arts and crafts, creative drama, puppet plays, movement, poetry, and writing. Patterns are also included with puppet plays and craft ideas.

This book is meant as a starting point for those who are interested in sharing quality literature with children. It is not an exhaustive source of author information— excellent sources such as *Children's Literature Review* and *Something About the Author* (Gale Research) may be used for further information. This resource does contain a few unique facts about each author and their works that provide a "hook" to get the children interested books.

The activities, chants, and discussion information are intended as literature-extension activities that will make the book sharing experience more memorable and meaningful to the young child. Each section can be used independently as a one session author program, or as an introduction to a more intensive author study.

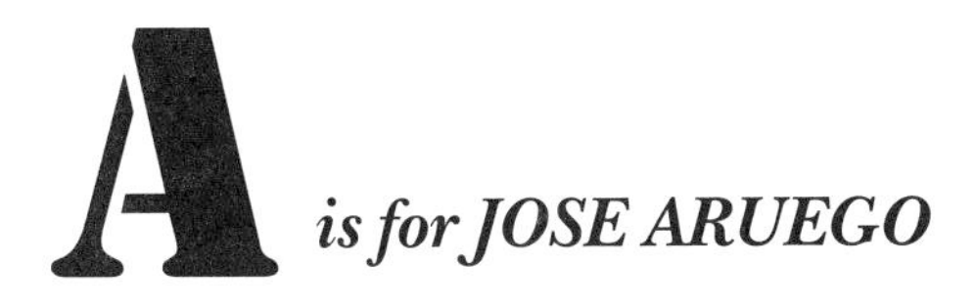

A is for JOSE ARUEGO

JOSE ARUEGO was born August 9, 1932, in Manila, Philippines. He attended college at the University of the Philippines finishing with a law degree. Mr. Aruego's father was a lawyer, and so were other members of his family. He tried being a lawyer, but he only had one case, which he lost. Believing his talents lay in an artistic field, Jose Aruego decided to follow his heart by attending Parsons School of Design where he studied graphic art. His illustrations reflect his graphical and cartoon-like style, especially the pen and ink drawings of humorous animals. Many of his books are co-authored with Ariane Dewey, to whom he was married for several years.

Mr. Aruego likes animals. At one time he had three horses, seven dogs, six cats, chickens, pigeons, frogs, ducks and three pigs. About his animal drawings, Mr. Aruego says "Children ask 'How do you draw funny animals?'" and he replies, "When I was in the first grade, everyone would say 'Jose Aurego is the best draw-er in the school.'" Ever since that time, he has been drawing.

Before Sharing Books

Discuss piranha and crocodiles. A piranha is a fish with very sharp teeth that lives in the Amazon area. They are only fourteen inches long, but a school of piranha can eat a 100-pound animal in one minute!

Crocodiles are found all over the world. They swim by swishing their strong tails back and forth and steer with their webbed feet. Crocodiles have interesting teeth— when old teeth wear out, they can grow new ones.

Books to Share

A Crocodile's Tale: A Philippine Folk Story. Scribners, 1972. The crocodile tries to eat Juan, but is tricked by a monkey.

Pilyo the Piranha. Macmillan, 1971. Pilyo is a very hungry piranha that will eat almost anything.

Rockabye Crocodile. Greenwillow, 1988. Two old boars with contrasting dispositions take turns babysitting a crocodile. These two find out that your attitude towards a job makes all the difference in the world.

We Hide, You Seek. Greenwillow, 1979. Animals in East Africa teach about camouflage in this cheerful and colorful story. *Booklist* Starred Book, ALA Notable Book, 1979.

Warm-Up Activities

Chant

Crocodile Pool

I went to the crocodile pool,
Where the crocodiles think it's cool
Because they don't follow rules.
They stayed on the bottom,
And all that arose
Was just a great big crocodile nose.

Action Rhyme

Crocodile's Tale

Juan, basket, hat and monkey in a tree
(Raise arms like a tree)
That old crocodile can't catch me!
(Shake head "no" and point to self)
Croc snaps the basket,
(Clap on the word "snap")

Croc snaps the hat
But Juan and monkey weren't caught in the trap!
(Shake head "no" again)

Follow-Up Activities

Crocodile Mural

Materials: Blue butcher paper; green, black, white, red, and brown paint; pencils; glue and cups cut from paper (not styrofoam) egg cartons.

Directions: Enlarge the pattern and trace on blue butcher paper, copying as many crocodiles as you would like on your mural. Glue the cups of egg cartons to the crocodiles backs for a 3-D effect. Let the children paint the crocodiles with the paint.

Crocodile Key Chain

Materials: For each key chain, you will need a screw-type eye hook, a wooden doll clothespin (not the spring type), and white and red felt. You will also need a green and a black marker, scissors and glue.

Directions: Color the clothespin green with the marker. Screw the eye hook into the top end of the clothespin. Cut white felt teeth and eyes, and a red felt tongue. Glue the teeth on one leg of the clothespin, and glue one eye on each side. Glue the felt tongue in between the clothespin legs. Use the black marker to put in nostrils, pupils and other details. Attach to a key ring or to a zipper pull. Use the illustration below as a sample.

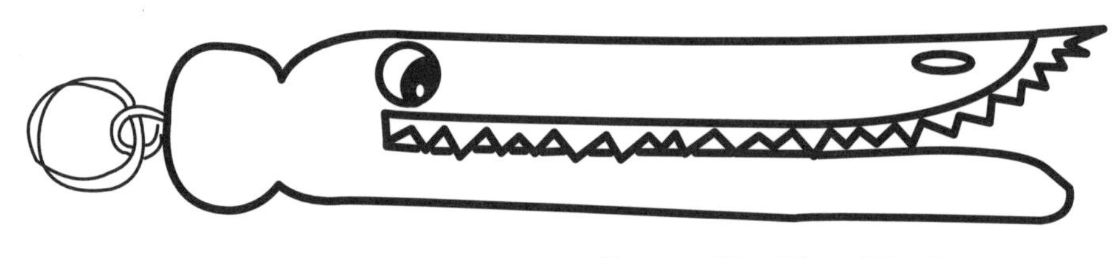

Crocodile Key Chain

Crocodile Mural

B is for JAN BRETT

JAN BRETT is known for her wonderfully detailed illustrations and simply told stories. Many of the stories she has written, be they original or retellings, focus on the relationships between animals and children. Ms. Brett was born on December 1, 1949, in Highham, Massachusetts. She had wanted to be an illustrator of children's books since she was a child.

Her pictures are watercolor and line, and feature authentic looking "Old World" folklore motifs in the architecture and clothing. In one of her books, *The Twelve Days of Christmas,* Ms. Brett chose items and styles from eleven European countries to help convey the story of the traditional carol. Many of her books also have ornamental borders that preview the action to take place on the next pages. For example, in *Annie and the Wild Animals*, the borders give glimpses of the next animal that will come to Annie's small cottage.

Ms. Brett still lives in Massachusetts where she likes to ride horses and go gliding.

Before Sharing Books

Gather together informational books that have pictures of traditional Bavarian and Scandinavian dress and decoration. Compare and contrast these pictures with the illustrations and border decorations in the books of Jan Brett. Be sure and point out where these countries are on a globe or map.

Books to Share

Annie and the Wild Animals. Houghton Mifflin, 1985. When Annie's cat disappears, she tries to make friends with a series of unsuitable woodland animals.

Berlioz the Bear. Putnam, 1991. The world of music is introduced through delightful bear characters set in Bavaria.

Goldilocks and the Three Bears. Putnam, 1987. The traditional tale of the lost little girl in the woods and the three suspicious bears.

The Mitten. Putnam, 1989. Several sleepy animals crawl snugly into Mickey's lost white mitten and all is well. Then the bear sneezes!

Warm-Up Activities

Chant

Teach the children this chant in German about a cat that goes out into the snow like the cat in *Annie and the Wild Animals.*

ABC Die Katze Lief Im Schnee

ABC, die katze lief im schnee
Und als sie dann nach hause kam
Da hatt sie weisse stiefel an
ABC, de katze lief im schnee!

Song

Bavarian Snow Song

There is a friend of mine
You might know him too.
Wears a derby hat—
He's real cool!

Has coal black eyes
An orangy carrot nose
Two funny stick arms
And an overcoat of snow.

Have you guessed his name
Or do you need a clue?
You'll never see his face
In summer or spring, guess who?
(Snowman)

Follow-Up Activity

Creative Dramatics

Dramatize the book *The Mitten* using the patterns provided. Children can either pantomime or repeat their parts as the story is read. Any extra children can be the important "Aaaahchoo!" in the story. A white knitted shawl or blanket works well as the mitten—children wrap themselves in it as each animal enters the warm shelter of the mitten.

Additional Selected Books by Jan Brett

Beauty and the Beast. Clarion, 1989. A retelling of this classic tale with Jan Brett's interpretation through wonderful illustrations.

Fritz and the Beautiful Horses. Houghton Mifflin, 1981. Fritz is a pony who is excluded from a clique of the city's most beautiful horses. He demonstrates that looks aren't everything when he rescues the city children.

Town Mouse, Country Mouse. Putnam, 1994. After trading houses, the two mice discover there is no place like home in this Christmas story.

Trouble with Trolls. Putnam, 1992. Treva outwits the trolls from Mount Baldy who are trying to kidnap her dog.

C *is for DONALD CREWS*

DONALD CREWS is an African American author who uses his training as a graphic designer to create books with poster-style graphics. His books have focused on such topics as transportation, motion, the alphabet and numbers, and they often use vivid colors. Mr. Crews simple and easily identifiable objects and characters have a special appeal to children.

Donald Crews was born on August 30, 1938, in New Jersey. He first worked as a photographer and illustrator for *Dance Magazine* and Will Burton Studios. He then turned to a career in children's book illustration after the publication of *We Read—A to Z* in 1967. In 1978 Crews achieved national recognition with the book *Freight Train,* a Caldecott Honor Book. He is married to Ann Jonas, who is also a children's author/illustrator.

Before Sharing Books

Discuss motion and movement. All of Donald Crews' books feature vehicles or objects that move. Use the book *Make It Go* by David Evans and Claudette Williams (Dorling Kindersley, 1992) to do some simple movement experiments.

Books to Share

Carousel. Greenwillow, 1982. A merry-go-round ride is described through a narrative study of light, shape and movement through collage and photography. ALA Notable Book, 1982.

Harbor. Greenwillow, 1982. All the color and action of loners, tugs, barges, ferryboats and fireboats in a harbor are presented in this visual story. *School Library Journal* Starred Book.

Parade. Greenwillow, 1983. Enjoy the fun and anticipation of watching a parade pass on these dynamic, colorful pages. *Booklist* Starred Book.

Shortcut. Greenwillow, 1992. The train tracks ran right by Bigmama's house in Cottondale, and the children were warned to stay off of them. But late one night, they decide to take a shortcut on the tracks. When a train comes, there was no turning back. *Booklist* Starred Book, *Publisher's Weekly* Starred Book.

Warm-Up Activities

Chant

I'm a Freight Train

I'm a freight train
Chugging down the track
A freight train
Going up and back.

I travel all day long
Going round and round
Taking merchant goods
From town to town to town.

I'm a freight train
Chugging down the track
A freight train
Going up and back
Chug-chug-chug-chug-*whooo!*

Rhyme

Carousel

Ride with me on the carousel
Round and round and round
Up and up the horses go
Then the horses go down.

Your horse is white
My horse is brown
Up and down on the carousel
Round and round and round.

Follow-Up Activity

Carousels!

Make these festive decorations after sharing *Carousel.*

Materials: For each child, you will need the animal patterns, construction paper, scissors, tape, coffee filters, glue, crayons, liquid watercolor paint, eyedroppers and ribbon scraps.

Directions: Have each child color and cut out their selected carousel animals from the patterns provided. Then glue the animals to a sheet of construction paper. After the glue dries, roll the paper so the ends meet and tape them together to form a cylinder that will stand on its end (See sample below). Each child can now take a coffee filter and decorate it by dripping the liquid watercolors using the eyedroppers. When the filters are dry, glue them on top of the cylinder to form a canopy. Attach ribbon with tape to hang down the sides if desired.

Additional Selected Books by Donald Crews

Bigmama's. Greenwillow, 1991. When the train arrives in Cottondale, summer at Bigmama's house begins. A childhood experience conveyed realistically in this book. *Booklist* Starred Book.

Bicycle Race. Greenwillow, 1985. A counting book filled with suspense, motion and excitement as twelve cyclists compete in a race.

Flying. Greenwillow, 1986. A plane journey captured with minimal text and maximal color.

School Bus. Greenwillow, 1984. Crisp yellow illustrations tell the story of the school bus' daily trips across town and to school. *School Library Journal* Starred Book.

Carousel

Carousel Animals

D is for *LULU DELACRE*

LULU DELACRE was born on December 20, 1957, in Puerto Rico. There she grew up surrounded by with her Argentinean family. Ms. Delacre remembers playing at her grandmother's house as a child, and drawing lots of pictures while there. She also remembers having lots of small creatures around to play with—a canary, two turtles, and several chicks. There were always lots of lizards and bugs around her home in the tropics too. She especially liked the lizards, whose mouths would open wide—she would then put them on her ears and pretend were earrings! She took drawing lessons at age ten, and from that time knew she wanted to be an artist.

Ms. Delacre studied at the University of Puerto Rico and then attended the Superior Graphic Arts College in Paris. There she learned about design, illustration and typography. She also saw an exhibit of artwork by Maurice Sendak that made her want to become a children's book illustrator.

Before Sharing Books

Using books such as *America the Beautiful: Puerto Rico* (Deborah Kent, Children's Press, 1992), discuss Puerto Rico and point out its location on the map. Talk about famous Puerto Ricans from many different disciplines—Pablo Casals, Roberto Clemente, Jose Feliciano and Raul Julia. This will be a good segue into the topic of Lulu Delacre.

Books to Share

Arroz Con Leche: Popular Songs and Rhythms from Latin America. Scholastic, 1990. A unique and wonderfully illustrated selection of bilingual music and nursery rhymes.

Bossy Gallito. Scholastic, 1994. A Cuban cumulative folktale in which the sun sets off a chain reaction that ends with the cleaning of a rooster's dirty beak.

Las Navidades. Scholastic, 1989. A celebration of family Christmas traditions in a Latin American community.

Nathan's Fishing Trip. Scholastic, 1989. Nathan is a childlike elephant who has many adventures. This book is one of the Nathan series.

Vejigantes Masquerade. Scholastic, 1993. Ramon finds a way to join the Vejigantes, masqueraders who parade through town during Carnaval, even after a feisty goat eats his costume.

Warm-Up Activities

Chant

Vejigantes Estribillos

Tun-tun-tun-eco
Let the trickster do a dance-o!

Toco-toco-toco nut
Vejigante loves coconut!

Rhyme

Masquerade

It's masquerade today
Let's celebrate this way
Clap our hands and shout "Ole!"
It's masquerade today!

Repeat with "stomp our feet," "circle our arms," and "circle around" in place of "clap our hands."

Rhyme

Carnaval

Here is Carnaval
What a sight to see
We are dressed in costumes
Just for you and me.

When Carnaval is over
We will circle around
Take off our masks
And jump up and down.

Follow-Up Activity

Masquerade Movement

Vejigantes are good-natured tricksters who play pranks during the month of February during the Puerto Rican Carnaval. *Vejigantes* hold painted balloons traditionally made from cow bladders called *vejigas,* hence the name *Vejigantes.* Let the children hold real balloons and color them with markers. They can then pretend to parade around, chase each other, shake their balloons and dance wild dances like the masqueraders.

E is for LOIS EHLERT

LOIS EHLERT has created delightfully illustrated picture books that introduce kids to gardening, shapes, counting, the alphabet and nature. She has designed many different types of things too—toys, games, books, banners, theater sets and even a reading program for the state of Wisconsin.

As a child, Ms. Ehlert credits the encouragement she received in art to her mother and father. In a home filled with sewing and woodworking, she had her own little workspace on a table that she still uses. Ms. Ehlert received training at the Layton School of Art, and then went on to become both a teacher and graphic artist. Her books are filled with eye-catching colors and shapes. Many of the illustrations are based on real objects and use collage, die cuts, painting and natural objects like sticks and leaves. Her books have won numerous awards, from a Caldecott Honor for *Color Zoo*, to Outstanding Science Trade Book for *Color Farm* and *Planting a Rainbow*.

Before Sharing Books

Discuss collage and the unique way it is used in Lois Ehlert's books. The book *Collage* by Sue Stocks (Thompson Learning, 1994) will help you define and explain the art of collage. Show examples of other picture books illustrated with collage such as those by Eric Carle or Ezra Jack Keats. Bring photos and real samples of fruit and vegetables. Compare these to the illustrations in Lois Ehlert's books. After comparing, cut up the real samples and serve with toothpick forks.

Books to Share

Eating the Alphabet: Fruits and Vegetables from A to Z. Harcourt Brace Jovanovich, 1989. Full-color fruits and vegetables teach upper and lower case letters to preschoolers. Includes a glossary of food facts. Parent's Reading Magic Award, *Booklist* Starred Books, *Kirkus Reviews* Starred Book, Printing Industries of America (PIA) Award.

Growing Vegetable Soup. Harcourt Brace Jovanovich, 1987. The gardening cycle is presented with fresh, bright illustrations and an easy recipe for vegetable soup. *Kirkus Reviews* Starred Book.

Planting a Rainbow. Harcourt Brace Jovanovich, 1992. This educational book helps children understand how to plant bulbs, seeds and seedlings, and then nurture their growth.

Red Leaf, Yellow Leaf. Harcourt Brace Jovanovich, 1991. Watercolor and collage pieces of actual seeds, fabric, wire and roots illustrate the life of a tree. A glossary explains photosynthesis, root absorption, sap circulation and other tree facts. *Booklist* Starred Book, *Hornbook* Starred Book, *Kirkus Review* Starred Book, PIA Award.

Warm-Up Activities

Chant

Out In the Garden (To the tune of "Down by the Station")

Out in the garden
Early in the morning
See the _________ _________ all in a row
Here we go to pick them
Then we will eat them
Pick, pick, eat, eat,
Off we go.

(Fill in blank with desired vegetables and colors.)

Follow-Up Activities

Vegetable Paper Chains

Materials: Each child will need a pencil, and 8½" x 11" piece of colored paper, and scissors.

Directions: Fold the colored paper in half lengthwise to get a 5½" x 8" rectangle. Have children fold each edge back towards the center fold. This creates the fan fold that makes the paper chain work. Using the vegetable patterns provided, have students select and cut out the shape of their choice. Then place the shape over the folded paper so that each side overlaps the edges. Trace around the outside of the shape onto the paper. Cut out the shape, being careful to leave the folded edges intact. Unfold to reveal the vegetable chain.

Alphabet Books

Follow Lois Ehlert's example in the book *Eating the Alphabet* and have the children compile their own food alphabet book—let them choose the topic, such as junk food, desserts or multicultural food. Children can illustrate or use pictures cut from magazines to make collages of each food. Be sure to add a glossary of foods in the back just as Ms. Ehlert did!

Additional Selected books by Lois Ehlert

Feathers for Lunch. Harcourt Brace Jovanovich, 1990. An escaped house cat encounters twelve backyard birds but ends up with only feathers for lunch. A bird guide is included. Association International of Graphic Arts (AIGA) Award, *Horn Book* Starred Book.

Fish Eyes: A Book You Can Count On. Harcourt Brace Jovanovich, 1990. Brightly colored fish introduce young readers to counting and basic addition. *Booklist* Starred Book, Printing Industries of America Award.

Mole's Hill: A Woodland Tale. Harcourt Brace Jovanovich, 1994. Mole has a lovely home by the pond, but Fox orders her to move to make room for a new garden path. Artwork inspired by Woodland Indians ribbon applique and beadwork. *Hornbook* Starred Book, *Publisher's Weekly* Starred Book.

Nuts to You. Harcourt Brace Jovanovich, 1993. A squirrel is busy digging, hiding, and zipping. After he sneaks into an apartment house, how will he get out? A glossary of squirrel facts and identification labels on each page. *Booklist* Starred Book, *Publisher's Weekly* Starred Book.

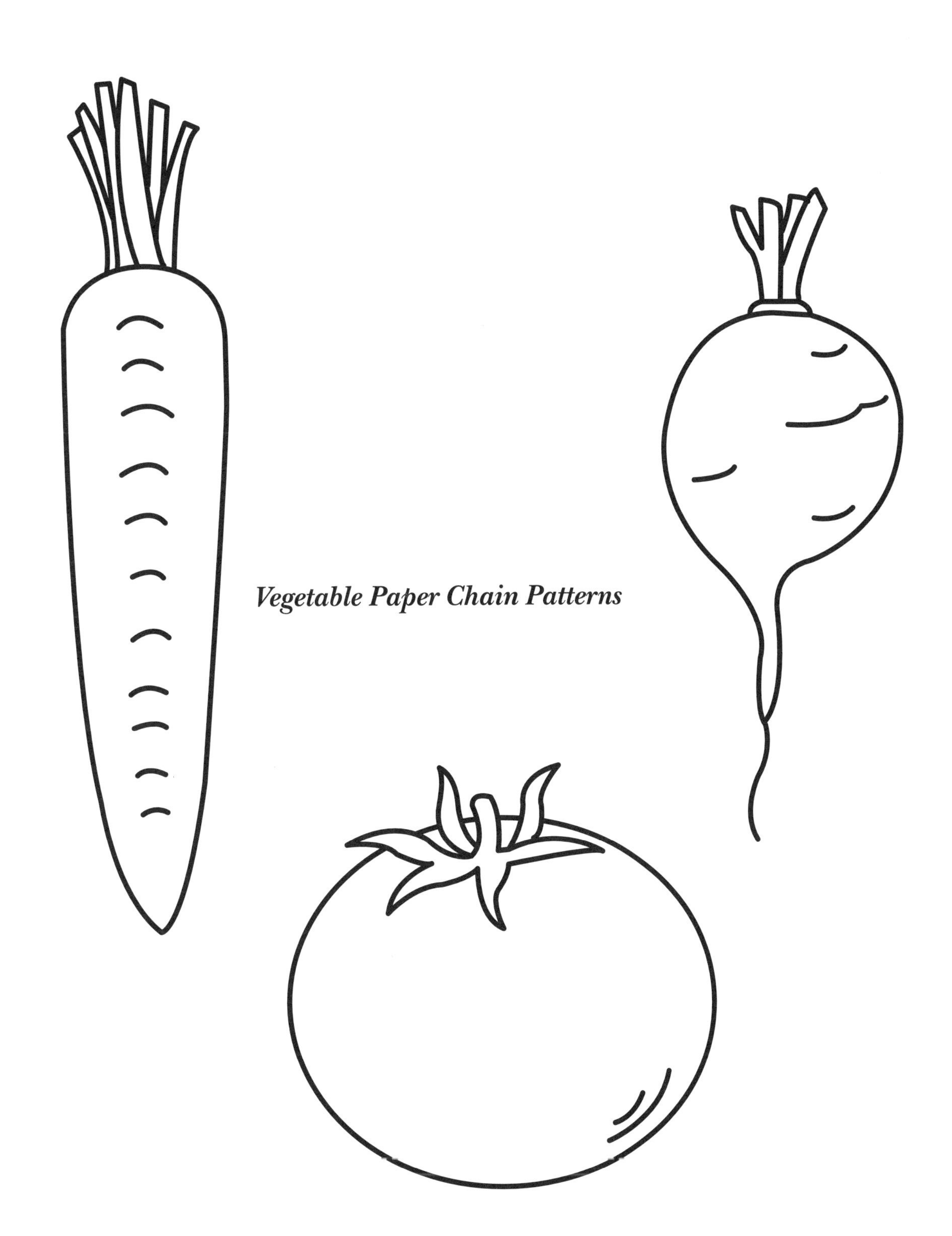
Vegetable Paper Chain Patterns

F is for DENISE FLEMING

DENISE FLEMING, author and illustrator of *In the Tall, Tall Grass,* a 1994 Caldecott Honor book, stands out as one of the only children's book illustrators to create artwork for her books in handmade paper. Ms. Fleming uses cotton rag fiber to create "pulp paintings."

Ms. Fleming has worked for ad agencies, toy companies, and even designed furniture and lunch boxes. She started out illustrating other people's stories, but sometimes had a hard time visualizing their ideas. She would make miniature dolls of the characters in the stories to help her illustrate. Then she began to write as well as illustrate books, and chose subjects that she liked, such as nature, colors and wild creatures. Speaking at a recent library conference, Ms. Fleming said, "This is nature through my eyes, so it is not exact. What they convey is the mood or feeling of being in the story—Skies are not yellow, but a yellow sky conveys the feeling of a hot summer afternoon. So I used a yellow sky in *In the Tall, Tall Grass.*" Ms. Fleming also likes to use words that kids like to say. Since she and her husband design all of her books, including mechanicals, placement and type, she is able to incorporate the words as part of her pictures. Ms. Fleming says the art that has had the greatest influence on her own is children's art. She even has two giant murals that children painted hanging in her hallway.

Ms. Fleming lives in Toledo,Ohio, with her husband and daughter. She confided to a Texas audience, "I love armadillos, and my license plate says TEX-493, even though I live in Ohio."

Before Sharing Books

Use the book *Paper* by Annabelle Dixon (Garrett, 1991), to explain how paper is made from wood at a mill. Contrast this with the method of making paper by hand from recycled paper pulp that Denise Fleming uses.

Books to Share

Barnyard Banter. Henry Holt, 1994. Rhythms, rhymes and animal sounds abound in this barnyard tour.

Count. Henry Holt, 1992. *Publisher's Weekly* Best Book. The antics of lively and colorful animals present the numbers one to ten, twenty, thirty, forty, and fifty.

In the Small, Small Pond. Henry Holt, 1993. Text and illustration show small animals that live in ponds from spring to autumn. A frog is pictured on each page. Caldecott Honor Book, *School Library Journal* Best Book, ALA Notable Book.

In the Tall, Tall Grass. Henry Holt, 1993. Rhymed text presents a bug's eye view of animals found in the grass from lunchtime to nightfall. ALA Notable Book, *School Library Journal* Best Book, *Horn Book* Honor Book, International Reading Assn.–Children's Book Club (IRA–CBC) Children's Choice, NCTE Notable Book in the Language Arts.

Lunch. Henry Holt, 1992. A very hungry mouse eats a large lunch of colorful foods. *School Library Journal* Starred Book.

Warm-Up Activities

Chant

To use with In the Tall, Tall Grass. (To the tune of "Frere Jacques")

Big bugs, small bugs,
Big bugs, small bugs,
See them crawl
In the grass
Creepy creepy crawling

Never, ever falling
Bugs, bugs, bugs
Creep, creep, crawl.

Song

Barnyard Sounds (To the tune of "The Wheels on the Bus"). Use with Barnyard Banter.

The cow in the barn goes moo, moo, moo;
Moo, moo, moo, moo, moo, moo.
The cow in the barn goes moo, moo, moo,
All around the farm.

Repeat with "The pig in the pen goes oink oink oink," "The rooster on the fence goes cock-a-doodle-doo," etc.

Follow-Up Activity

Cookie Cutter Paper

Materials: Construction paper torn into small pieces (divided by color); an embroidery hoop, fiberglass window screen, dishcloths, dishpan, two sticks to hold the paper screen over the dishpan, a blender, plastic cups to hold wet pulp, water, cookie cutters, newspaper, plain scrap paper, and a sponge.

Directions: Stretch the screen over the embroidery hoop as you would fabric to make a paper screen. Place the dishtowels on top of a pile of newspapers to make a "couching" pile.* Put 1⁄3 cup firmly packed construction paper of the same color into a blender. Fill the blender two-thirds full with water. Blend for 60 seconds or until pulp is slurry.

Place paper screen on sticks over dishpan with the screen side up. Put a cookie cutter on top of the screen and pour pulp inside until it is as least ⅛" thick. Very carefully remove cookie cutter after water has drained through. Flip the paper screen on top of the couching pile with the pulp-side down. Remove screen and cover cookie-cutter paper shape with another dishcloth. Sponge off excess water. Now flip the pulp onto your plain scrap paper, and place another plain paper over it. Weight it, and let dry for several days.

For a special touch, add glitter or embroidery floss. Poke a hole in the shape when it is dry to allow it to hang.

*A ***couching pile*** (pronounced cooching) is a stack of dry materials that help absorb the excess water from handmade paper.

G is for PAUL GOBLE

PAUL GOBLE is an English author and illustrator who has successfully retold many Native American legends and myths in picture-book format. Goble's books are unique in that they blend his own personal artistic style in a very harmonious way with the stories he preserves. It is interesting to note that Goble bases his unique method of watercolor painting on actual Native American artwork made by captive Indians in the 1870s as well as on his own formal training. For example, symbols portrayed as wavy lines representing lightning are used alongside very modern composition and design.

Goble was born in Haslemere, England on September 27, 1933. It was there that he became interested in Native American culture after he received a copy of the book *Notes on the North American Indian* by George Catlin. Mr. Goble studied Native Americans informally while pursuing a degree in industrial design. He was a designer and teacher until 1977, when he decided to move to South Dakota and take up writing and illustrating full time. The Sioux Indians have adopted Goble as part of their tribe and call him "Little Thunder."

Before Sharing Books

Discuss trickster tales from many cultures. Some tricksters to learn about arc Iktomi, from thc Lakota Indian tradition; Anansi, African and Brer Rabbit, who is part of the tradition of the southern U.S. Compare Anansi and Brer Rabbit to Iktomi using books such as *Anansi and the Moss Covered Rock* by Eric Kimmel (Holiday House, 1988) and *Jump!* by Parks Van Dyke (Harcourt Brace Jovanovich, 1985).

Books to Share

Iktomi and the Berries: A Plains Indian Story. Orchard Watts, 1989. Iktomi tries and tries to pick buffalo berries.

Iktomi and the Boulder. Orchard Watts, 1991. Iktomi tries to outwit a boulder with the help of some bats in this explanation of why the Great Plains are covered with small stones. ALA Notable Children's Book, *Parent's Magazine* Reading Magic Award, Notable Children's Social Studies Book (NCSS-CBC).

Iktomi and the Buzzard. Orchard Watts, 1994. Iktomi tries to trick Buzzard into giving him a ride across the river on Buzzard's back.

Iktomi and the Ducks. Orchard Watts, 1990. After outwitting some ducks, Iktomi is outwitted by Coyote.

Warm-Up Activities

Chant

Native American chants below and on p. 25 are pronounced exactly as written.

Deer Chant (Chippewa)

Tee bee wen da ba no gwen, eye ya bay
Tee bee wen da ba no gwen, eye ya bay
Eye ya bay, eye ya bay.

(Whence does he spring, the deer
Whence does he spring, the deer
The deer, the deer.)

Song

Duck Dance (Apache)
(to the tempo of a beating drum)

He ha ya li noo, he ha ya li noo,
He ha ya li noo, he ha ya li noo,
He ha ya we heya, heya,
We heya, heya, we heya, heya
We heya, heya, we heya, heya.
Ya koi he! Ya koi he!
Hah, Kah, kah, kah!

Follow-Up Activity

Writing

Have your group create its own Iktomi tale. The pattern these stories follow has Iktomi trying to trick an animal or object but ending up being tricked himself. For example, write and illustrate "Iktomi and the Snake," where Iktomi tries to trick the snake out of its lovely skin to make a fine belt, but ends up with a snake shedding instead.

Additional Books by Paul Goble

The Girl Who Loved Wild Horses. Macmillan, 1982. Caldecott Medal. A young girl loves her people, but only feels truly free and happy among the wild horses.

The Great Race. Macmillan, 1985. A retelling of a Cheyenne and Sioux myth about a contest between man and buffalo to see who would have supremacy over all.

I Sing for the Animals. Macmillan, 1991. A reflection of how we are all connected on this earth and connected to our creator.

Love Flute. Macmillan, 1992. A shy young man is unable to express his love to a beautiful maiden until he receives a gift from the birds and animals.

H is for KEVIN HENKES

KEVIN HENKES funny picture books feature animal characters that face familiar childhood dilemmas such as sibling rivalry, starting school, boredom and friendships. Henkes was born in Racine, Wisconsin, in 1960 and still lives there today. He has always been a writer and illustrator, and seems to have a special knack for presenting situations as they would occur to children. His most popular books present young mice as the cheerful and amusing protagonists. Mr. Henkes first book, All Alone, was accepted for publication when he was nineteen. Perhaps having a book published at such a young age has added to his ability to understand the fears and dilemmas of childhood. He translates these universal concerns, such as not liking one's name (*Chrysanthemum*) into wonderful stories.

Before Sharing Books

Discuss childhood situations that are sometimes hard, such as not wanting to go to school, new kids in class, disliking your name, etc. Introduce the books by Kevin Henkes that have some of these problems in them.

Books to Share

Chester's Way. Greenwillow, 1988. Chester and Wilson are best friends, and also very set in their ways, that is, until Lilly moves into the neighborhood. *School Library Journal* Starred Book.

Chrysanthemum. Greenwillow, 1991. Chrysanthemum loves her name—until the day she starts school. The other mice make fun of her long name. *School Library Journal* Starred Book, ALA Notable Book, 1991, *Horn Book* Starred Book.

Owen. Greenwillow, 1993. Owen just loves his yellow blanket. He takes it with him everywhere. Now it is time for Owen to start school, and everyone tries plots to get rid of his blanket, but Owen foils them all. *Booklist* Starred Book, *School Library Journal* Starred Book, ALA Notable Book, 1993, Caldecott Honor Book, 1994, *Horn Book* Award Honor Book, 1994.

Sheila Rae, the Brave. Greenwillow, 1987. Sheila Rae the mouse is fearless. Her little sister, Louise, is the scared mouse. Then one day, Sheila Rae gets lost and it is Louise to the rescue. *School Library Journal* Starred Book.

Warm-Up Activities

Chant

Magalena Hagalena, a Very Unusual Girl

Magalena Hagalena
Ooka Taka Waka Taka
Oka Moka Poka was her name.

She had two teeth
In the middle of her mouth
One pointed north
One pointed south.
(Repeat first verse)

She had two eyes
In the middle of her head
One was green
The other was red.
(Repeat first verse)

She had ten hairs
Hanging down
Five were orange
And the rest were brown.
(Repeat first verse)

Action Rhyme

Friends

My friends, over the way,
My friends, over the way,
My friends, over the way,
Come and skip with me today!

(Repeat, substituting walk, run, hop, wave, smile, etc., for the word "skip." Suit actions to words.)

Follow-Up Activity

Peanut Mice

For this activity, children will create one of the lovable mice in Kevin Henkes stories using a peanut.

Materials: Each child will need one peanut in the shell, 2½ brown pipe cleaners, scissors, glue, brown and pink felt scraps, and markers.

Directions: Have children wrap one pipe cleaner around the center of the peanut to form arms. Poke holes in the bottom of the peanut and insert the other pipe cleaner through. Secure it with a drop of glue. Cut two circles from the brown felt, and two smaller circles from the pink felt. Glue the pink circles on top of the brown circles. Glue the circles to the top of the peanut's head to make ears. Poke another hole in the bottom of the peanut and insert the ½ pipe cleaner to make a tail. Then have children draw a face on their peanut mouse with a marker.

Additional Selected books by Kevin Henkes

Bailey Goes Camping. Greenwillow, 1985. Bailey is too young to go camping with the Bunny Scouts, but Mama and Papa show him how to camp right at their own house.

Clean Enough. Greenwillow, 1982. The narrator sits in his bath playing, remembering, pretending—doing anything but washing.

Granpa and Bo. Greenwillow, 1986. Bo spends a wonderful summer in the country with his Grandpa, walking, talking, fishing and laughing.

Jessica. Greenwillow, 1989. A shy preschooler insists her friend Jessica is not imaginary, and in the end she is absolutely right. *School Library Journal* Starred Book, *Horn Book* Starred Book.

Julius, the Baby of the World. Greenwillow, 1990. Julius, Lilly's baby brother is nothing but dreadful. *School Library Journal* Starred Book, *Horn Book* Starred Book.

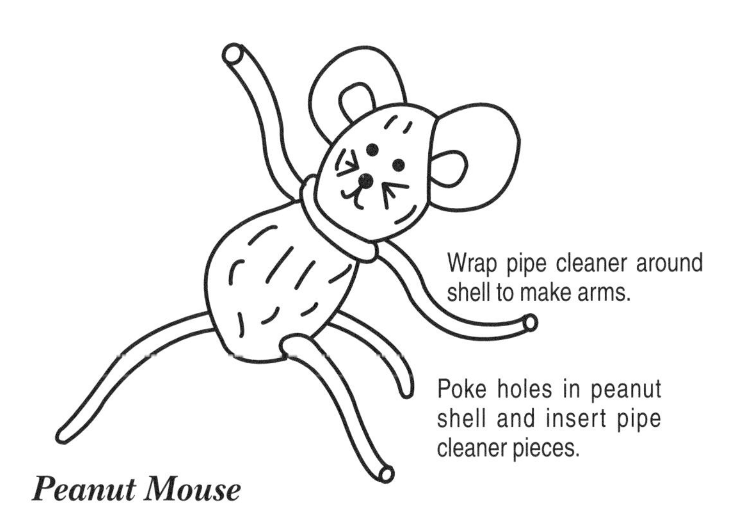
Wrap pipe cleaner around
shell to make arms.
Poke holes in peanut
shell and insert pipe
cleaner pieces.

Peanut Mouse

Ear pattern

I *is for SATOMI ICHIKAWA*

SATOMI ICHIKAWA was born in Gifu, Japan, on January 15, 1949. She was unsure of what she wanted to do with her life, so in college she took a general course of study. Ichikawa thought she would finish school and then get married and not work. But one summer she took a trip to Paris and fell in love with France. She decided to stay and worked as a children's nanny while studying French. In a small bookstore, she discovered a book illustrated by Maurice Boutet de Monvel. In finding that book, she found her calling and soon began to draw. Ms. Ichikawa had no formal training, but took her drawings to a publisher whose address she copied out of the front of a children's book—thus her first book, *A Child's Book of Seasons*, was published in 1946. Ms. Ichikawa continues to produce warm and wonderful books, all the while living in Paris in the same studio complex that was home to Pablo Picasso.

Before Sharing Books

Discuss children around the world. Have the children think about the things in the Nora books—animals, castles, stars, toys and her dog. Are these things common to children everywhere; are they things that the children in your group enjoy too? Ask the children if they have a favorite pet or toy they bring everywhere they go.

Books to Share

Nora's Castle. Putnam, 1986. Nora sets out to see the mysterious castle on the hill accompanied by Kiki the dog, Teddy the bear, and Maggie the doll.

Nora's Duck. Putnam, 1991. Nora finds a baby duck and takes it to Dr. John, who cares for many ill and abandoned animals.

Nora's Stars. Putnam, 1989. While visiting her grandmother, Nora joins with some toys from an old chest to bring the stars down from the sky. The stars absence soon make the sky dark and sad.

Nora's Surprise. Putnam, 1994. Nora's outdoor tea party with her toys at the home of some friendly geese is disrupted by Benji, a very greedy sheep from next door.

Warm-Up Activities

Song

(Tune of *Are You Sleeping*)

Nora is special
Nora is special
Look in the book, you will see
A very special person
A very special person
That is she,
That is she.

Chant

Nora's Duck

Nora found a tiny duck
Sitting all alone.
Poor little baby duck
Where is its home?

Nora and her three friends
Maggie and Kiki and Ted,
Took the duck to Dr. John
And he put it to bed!

Geese and ducks, turtles and hens,
Sheep, goats, and a donkey, too.
Dr. John takes care of them all
And makes them feel brand new!

Follow-Up Activity

Favorite Things Books

Have the children look through magazines and catalogs and cut out pictures of things that appeal to them. Make sure the pictures will fit into a ziplock sandwich bag. Let the children glue the pictures of their choice to construction paper of various colors. (Pre-cut the construction paper to fit into zip lock bags.) Put one page in each ziplock bag. Turn the bags into books by stapling together or by punching holes in the bags and then stringing them on yarn.

Additional Selected Books by Satomi Ichikawa

Bravo, Tanya. Putnam, 1992. Tanya loves to dance, but has trouble with counting steps until she follows the music in her head.

Fickle Barbara. Putnam, 1993. Ballerina Bear Barbara, who lives in a child's room in Paris, discovers that while making new friends is wonderful, old friends should not be forgotten.

Nora's Roses. Putnam, 1993. After watching other people pick roses outside her window while she is sick, Nora has a lovely dream about the flowers.

Rosy's Garden. Putnam, 1990. Rosy learns the facts and folklore of flowers while visiting her grandmother in the country.

J is for *TONY JOHNSTON*

TONY JOHNSTON was born on January 30, 1942, in Los Angeles, and grew up in San Marino, California. She often visited her grandfather on his ranch, and these experiences later became the basis for *Grandpa's Song* (Dial, 1991).

Ms. Johnston went to college at the University of California at Berkeley and Stanford University, where she was an education major. After graduating she became a school teacher. While teaching, a fellow teacher saw a story she had written for a fourth grade class and suggested she get it published. When her husband's job transfer took them to New York, she came a step closer to a career as a children's book author.

In New York, Ms. Johnston held various jobs in publishing, including the editing of children's books. While working at Harper and Row as a manuscript reader, she was able to learn about publishing children's books firsthand. She then became secretary to Ursula Nordstrom, a legendary children's book editor.

Ms. Johnston also lived for a time in Mexico City, where she wrote stories in Spanish. She collects handwoven Indian belts, and her goal in writing is to be a good storyteller.

Before Sharing books

Discuss memories and how they affect us. In the books *The Quilt Story, The Promise, Yonder,* and *The Cowboy and the Black-Eyed Pea,* memory has a role. Let the children predict what part the memories will play and check their predictions before and after sharing the books.

Books to Share

The Cowboy and the Black-Eyed Pea. Putnam, 1992. Farthee Well is a pretty young cowgirl with a big ranch. Now all she needs is a real cowboy!

The Promise. Harper Collins, 1992. While helping her neighbor assist in the birth of a baby calf, a young cow lover hears the long ago story of a boy who also was interested in cows.

The Quilt Story. Putnam, 1992. A pioneer mother lovingly stitches a quilt which comforts her daughter Abigail. Many years later, another mother patches the quilt to bring her daughter comfort also.

The Tale of Rabbit and Coyote. Putnam, 1994. Rabbit outwits coyote in this Zapotec tale about why coyote howls at the moon.

Yonder. Dial, 1988. As the plum tree changes with the passing seasons, so do the lives of three generations of a farm family.

Warm-Up Activities

Chant

Cowboy

A cowboy wears a western hat,
He rides a running horse.
He has a rope called a lariat
And shoots real straight of course.

Rhyme

Cowgirl

Salty is my father's horse
I ride him when I can.
My mother helped me saddle
And across the fields we run.

I feel just like a cowgirl
When I'm sitting way up high.
One day I'll ride him very fast
Under a clear blue sky.

Follow-Up Activity

Wrangler and Rattler Movement Game

Choose one child as the rattlesnake, and another as the wrangler. The rattler gets a maraca or container of beans to shake. The wrangler gets a sock filled with paper. Both are blindfolded and put in the center of a circle of the remaining children (the corral). The rattler shakes the maraca, and the wrangler must try to "rope" the rattler with the sock by touching them with it. When the wrangler ropes the rattler, then he chooses a new wrangler to take his place. The wrangler then may choose a new rattler.

Additional Selected Books by Tony Johnston

Lorenzo the Naughty Parrot. Harcourt Brace Jovanovich, 1992. Lorenzo is a green-as-a-leaf squawking parrot who lives in Mexico. Wherever the action—or cookies—are, that's where you'll find Lorenzo.

The Old Lady and The Birds. Harcourt Brace Jovanovich, 1994. The joys of a garden on a sunny day in Mexico are felt by an old lady, her cat and the birds.

Slither McCreep and His Brother Joe. Harcourt Brace Jovanovich, 1992. Sibling rivalry exists between snake brothers, Slither and Joe McCreep.

The Soup Bone. Harcourt Brace Jovanovich, 1990. Looking for a soup bone on Halloween, a little old lady finds a hungry skeleton instead. Association International of Graphic Arts (AIGA) Award.

K is for BERT KITCHEN

BERT KITCHEN is best known for his very detailed realistic drawings in books such as *Somewhere Today* and *Animal Alphabet.* Mr. Kitchen is originally from England, where he attended the London Central School of Arts and Crafts and began his career as a fine artist, who was successful in showing and exhibiting his work. He still has a focus on the fine arts and gives lectures on drawing at the London Polytechnic School.

He also worked in textile design and set paintings for films. His drawings are very meticulous, detailed and beautiful. Many of them contain unusual or little known facts about the animals he illustrates. Often, in fact, the animals themselves are rare and unusual, such as the pangolin (similar to the anteater and the armadillo, found in Asia, Indonesia, and Africa.) and the tenerec (hedgehog-like animal from Madagascar).

Before Sharing Books

Discuss realistic drawing. Show examples of other picture book artists who draw realistically, such as Jan Brett, and compare those to the art of Denise Fleming or Lois Ehlert, who are less realistic in approach.

Books to Share

And So They Build. Candlewick, 1993. Twelve animal architects are described, as well as how and why they build their homes.

Somewhere Today. Candlewick, 1992. Rituals of play, courtship and survival are described for twelve unusual acting animals.

When Hunger Calls. Candlewick, 1994. Beautiful acrylic paintings accompany text that explains how twelve predatory mammals, birds and insects capture and devour their food.

Warm-Up Activities

Chant

Animal Homes

A squirrel lives in a tree
A snail lives in a shell,
A bear lives in a cave
It suits them all quite well.
A fish lives in the ocean
A bird lives in a nest
And we live in a house
And our home is best.

Poem

Kindness to Animals

Listen, children, never give
Pain to things that feel and live;
Let the red robin come
For some crumbs you save at home,—
As his meal you throw along
He'll repay you with a song!
Never hurt a timid hare
Peeping from a green grass lair;
Let her come with you and play
In the yard for the day.
So as you happily go along
Don't do these gentle creatures wrong.

Follow-Up Activities

Animal Pairs Movement

After sharing the book *Somewhere Today,* have each child choose a partner. Mimic some of the movements made by the animals in this book. Or try choosing a child to mimic animals movements while the other children guess at the animal.

Additional Selected Books by Bert Kitchen

Animal Alphabet. Dial, 1984. The reader is invited to guess the identity of 26 unusual animals illustrating the letters of the alphabet.

Animal Numbers. Dial, 1987. Exotic and familiar animals are shown with a specified number of their babies.

Gorilla—Chinchilla. Dial, 1990. Rhymed text and pictures show a variety of animal pairs with different habitats and appearance.

Tenrec's Twigs. Putnam, 1989. Tenrec feels doubtful about the small twiggy structures he builds, so he asks a variety of animals for their opinions.

L is for JEANNE M. LEE

JEANNE M. LEE spent her childhood in Vietnam, and has travelled extensively throughout southeast Asia. She came to the United States and studied art at Newton College in Massachusetts. There, she received a BFA in painting and met her husband. She now lives in Lexington with her husband and two sons.

Ms. Lee illustrates her books in soft pastels, watercolors, and drawings. For the book *Silent Lotus,* she visited the twelfth-century temple at Angkor Wat in Cambodia. The illustrations in this book were inspired by the temple decorations. Many of her books share Vietnamese and Chinese folktales through the text and illustrations.

Before Sharing Books

Discuss Vietnam using Karen Jacobsen's *Vietnam* (Children's Press, 1992). The country's climate, geography and history make it a place that contrasts sharply with the United States. It has jungle and forest habitats that are filled with animals such as panthers, deer, monkey and elephants. Teak, mahogany, pine and oak are grown exportation. Its recent history has been shadowed by war, with 418,000 people fleeing post-war Vietnam to immigrate to the U.S. from 1976–1986. Discuss how Ms. Lee's country and travels might have influenced her choice of subject matter in her books.

Books to Share

Ba-Nam. Henry Holt, 1987. A young girl visiting her ancestor's graves is frightened by an old woman, until a storm shows the woman's kindness.

The Legend of the Li River. Henry Holt, 1983. The legend of the origin of the magical hills that line China's Li River.

The Legend of the Milky Way. Henry Holt, 1982. A love story about the Milky Way and a sky princess who came down from heaven to marry a mortal.

Toad is the Uncle of Heaven. Henry Holt, 1985. Toad leads a group of animals to ask the King of Heaven to send rain.

Silent Lotus. Henry Holt, 1987. Inspired by the decorations at a twelfth century temple, this book tells the story of a silent and deaf girl who wants to become a Cambodian court dancer.

Warm-Up Activities

Chant

Vietnamese Greetings

Hello	Ống mạnh giỏi khong (ong mang zoi knong)
I like you	Tố qủi ông lắm (toi kway ong lam)
Thank you	Cảm ỏn nhiêủ (cam on new)
Goodbye	Hẹn gặp lại (hen gap lay)

Action Rhyme

Toad's Rhyme

Dry, dry
Why so dry?
Find King of Heaven
And ask him why.

Toad told bees,
Rooster , too.
Next came Tiger
And a jump through the blue.

Dry, dry
Why so dry?
Find King of Heaven
And ask him why.

Follow-Up Activity

Bite the Carp's Tail Game

For this traditional Vietnamese game have children stand in a single-file line with each child's hands on the back of the person in front of them. The first person in line is the carp's head, and the last is the carp's tail. The head must try to "bite" the tail by grabbing hold. To avoid being "bitten," the tail will swing and coil the end of the line away from the head. But the children must hold tight, so the line will not break. When the tail is "bitten" the head goes to the end of the line and is the tail, while the second in line is the new head.

M *is for JAMES MARSHALL*

JAMES EDWARD MARSHALL was born in San Antonio, Texas, on October 10, 1942. Speaking at a conference in Texas, Mr. Marshall referred to his love for his native state by saying, "I was born practically in the Alamo, so I am about as Texan as you can get. I try to put a little bit of Texas in every book I do." He never went to art school, but did attend the New England Conservatory of Music and Southern Connecticut State College. Mr. Marshall's books have won many awards, both for illustrations and story, including the Caldecott Honor Book citation.

Many of his books have been made into animated films. The book *It's So Nice to Have a Wolf Around the House* was made into a full length cartoon feature and won the Academy Award for best animated film in 1978. Mr. Marshall's line drawings of favorite characters such as "George and Martha" "Miss Nelson," and "The Stupids" are known to kids all over the world.

Sadly, James Marshall passed away in 1992.

Before Sharing Books

Discuss fractured fairy tales—fairy tales with mixed up plots or surprise endings. The books below by James Marshall are slightly modernized and changed from the original tales. Some other examples to share are *The True Story of the Three Little Pigs* (Viking Kestrel, 1989) and *The Frog Prince Continued* (Viking, 1990) both by Jon Scieszka.

Books to Share

Goldilocks and the Three Bears. Dial, 1988. Three bears return home to find a little girl asleep in baby bear's bed.

Hansel and Gretel. Dial, 1990. A poor woodcutter's children lost in the woods come upon a lovely house made of cookies and candy that is home to a witch.

Red Riding Hood. Dial, 1987. The tale of a little girl and a big, bad wolf.

The Three Little Pigs. Dial, 1989. This book retells the familiar tale in which only one of three pig brothers survives the attack of a wolf through careful planning.

Warm-Up Activities

Chant

The Three Little Pigs ate the wolf
And Goldilocks scared the Bears!
Red Riding Hood has a new fur coat
And Gretel has eaten the stairs!

Song

"Little Pink Pig" from *Oh, The Animals* by David Williams (Trapdoor Records, 1990, cassette).

Action Rhyme

Who's That?

Howl, howl, thud, thud, *(slap floor)*
Roar, roar! *(roar out loud)*
Who's that knocking on the door?

Pound, pound, *(hit floor)*
stamp, stamp, *(stamp on floor)*
Scratch, scratch, *(make scratching motion)*
Who's that wiggling on the latch?
Can it be a pig visiting me? *(oink, oink)*
No, pigs don't howl you see!
Can it be Red Riding Hood wiggling my latch? *(giggle, giggle)*
No, I don't think Red would scratch.

Growl, growl,
Scratch, scratch,
Howl, howl!
It's not an owl. *(hoot, hoot)*

Hmm, I think I'll peek to see,
OH NO! It's the Big Bad Wolf visiting me!
(Throw arms up)

Follow-Up Activity

Puppet Show

Use the fractured fairy tale *The Perils of Piggy Pearl* (see page 38) for the children to perform. Make stick puppets and props by tracing the patterns provided on to poster board. Color the puppets and props with crayons or markers. Cut them out, and attach the puppets to dowels or craft sticks.

Additional Selected Books by James Marshall

George and Martha. Houghton, 1972. Two lovable hippos teach the meaning of friendship in five mini-stories.

Space Case. Dial, 1980. When a visitor from outer space comes to earth, it is mistaken for a trick-or-treater and then a robot.

The Stupids Die. Houghton, 1981. The Stupids are so dumb, they think they are dead when the lights go out!

What's the Matter With Carruthers? Houghton, 1972. Carruthers is a very grumpy bear, and his friends want him to get in a good mood. Little do they know, it's way past Carruther's hibernation bed time!

Wings: A Tale of Two Chickens. Viking, 1986. Harriet the chicken must save her foolish friend from the clutches of a wily fox.

Yummers! Houghton, 1973. Eugene Turtle takes Emily Pig on a long walk to help her lose weight, but they end up stopping every few minutes for a snack.

The Perils of Piggy Pearl Or the Adventures of a Pig with a Voracious Appetite: A Fractured Fairy Tale

by Robin Davis and Susan Allison

Puppets: See stick puppet patterns beginning on page 40.

Props: See prop patterns beginning on page 40.

Act One

(Piggy Pearl skips in, carrying basket prop, singing)

PIGGY PEARL:

> *"Over the river and through the woods*
> *To Granny's house I go!*
> *With a basket of goodies*
> *And lots of sweet treats*
> *Because Granny likes to eat—OH!*

(To audience)

Hi! My name is Piggy Pearl and I like to eat, too! Cookies and candy and cake... *YUM!* Boy, am I starving. I bet Granny wouldn't miss a few of these goodies! *(Crunch munch chew)* Here's Granny's house. Granny! Yoo-Hoo! It's me—your little grandpiggy.

(Wolf enters)

WOLF : Hello, Dear. So nice to eat... I mean see you.

PIGGY: Hi, Granny! My, my did you have plastic surgery?? What big eyes you have.

WOLF : The better to see you with, my dear.

PIGGY: Why, Granny! If you did have surgery, they messed up your nose. What a big nose you have.

WOLF : The better to smell you with, my dear, and I must say you smell yummy, yummy, yummy.

PIGGY: And Granny, have you been to the dentist? What big teeth you have!

WOLF: The better to...

PIGGY: Teeth! Hey, that reminds me. It's dinner time and I'm starving. Bye! *(Exits)*

WOLF: Oh, well. I wonder if the three little pigs are home. *(Exits)*

Act Two

Put up table and bowls prop.

PIGGY: Oh dear. It's time for dinner and I'm so hungry. I'm also so lost. But look! A table with three bowls on it. And they are full of porridge. Yum! I love porridge. I don't see anybody around. I think I'll just have a little bit. *(Eats out of first bowl) Owww!* This porridge is too hot. But I'm so hungry, I think I'll eat it anyway. *(Eats out of second bowl)* Hey, this porridge is too cold. I'm still hungry, so I'll eat it anyway. *(Eats out of third bowl) MMMMM!* This porridge is just right, so I'm going to eat it, too. That was so good. Now I'm *(Yawning)* ready for a nap. I'd better go home. Besides, I wouldn't want to miss dinner!

Act Three

Remove table, put up bridge prop.
(Piggy enters)

PIGGY: I wonder if this is the right way home? Should I go over this bridge? Look over there. I think I see an apple tree. An apple would make a perfect snack—I just love apples! *(Starts to cross bridge)*

(Troll pops up)

TROLL: Growl!

PIGGY: Who are you?

TROLL: I'm the mean old nasty Troll and I'm going to eat you. Growl!

PIGGY: Eat *me?* Are you kidding? I'm Piggy Pearl and I'm on my way to get a snack—you can't eat me, you grumpy old Troll.

TROLL: Oh, yeah?

PIGGY: Yeah! *(Hits Troll on nose and exits across bridge)*

TROLL: *Owwwwww!* Did you see that? That pig hit me on the nose. First that big goat last week, and now a pig. I think I'll move to another bridge. *(Exits)*

Act Four

Remove bridge and put up bed prop
(Piggy enters)

PIGGY: Hello again. Guess where I'm going to sleep tonight? Right here in this castle on this bed. Look at this bed. Have you ever seen such a *huge* bed in your entire life?? How am I going to get up there? Here goes. *(Struggles and grunts trying to climb up bed)* Whew! I made it. All that climbing sure has made me hungry and tired. But this bed is so uncomfortable. You would think a castle would have nice beds, but this feels like I'm sleeping on a bowling ball or a watermelon. What is under this bed?? I guess I'll have to climb down and look. *(Struggles down and falls—THUD)* Now let's see what is under this bed. Oh, look! Yum, yum! *(sounds of chewing and munching)* Guess what was under this bed? A pea! A nice green pea, and it was delicious—the perfect snack. I wonder if there are any more peas. I know—I'll go outside in the garden and look! Yummy, yummy ....*(exits).*

Act Five

Take down bed prop.

PIGGY: Well here is the garden. Do you see any peas?? I see some—right here! *Yum! (Begins to munch loudly)* Oh! Oh. no! I knocked the peas off into a well. What will I do. I'm so hungry. *Boo hoo hoo!*

(Frog enters)

FROG: Hello, little piggy! Ribbit! Why are your crying? Ribbit!

PIGGY: Oh, hello. I didn't know anyone was here. I'm crying because I knocked some peas into the well and I'm so hungry. Boo hoo!

FROG: Ribbit! Don't cry, Piggy. I'll get your peas for you if you do something for me. Ribbit!

PIGGY: Oh, thank you. I'll do anything, just get my peas before I faint from hunger! What do you want?

FROG: Ribbit! I'll get your peas if you...Ribbit!

PIGGY: What? What??

FROG: Ribbit! I"ll get your peas if you give me a kiss! Ribbit!

PIGGY: A kiss?? Oh, yick-yack-yuck! Kiss a frog? You're kidding, right?

FROG: No, I mean it—I'll get the peas if you kiss me. Ribbit!

PIGGY: Yuck! But I'm so hungry. Well, okay. Here goes—on the count of three. One. Two. Three. *(kisses frog)* Oh, yuck, yuck , yuck!

(Frog disappears and Prince Pig comes up)

PIGGY: Oh! Where did you come from?? Where's the frog? Where are my peas??

PRINCE: Ribbit! It's me. An evil witch cast a spell on me and turned me into a frog. But you broke the spell and turned me back into a Piggy Prince by kissing me.

PIGGY: I did? *Wow!*

PRINCE: Do you know what this means?

PIGGY: What?

PRINCE: We can be married and live happily ever after. But first, let's go get something to eat. I am so sick of flies.

PIGGY: Okay! Yummy, yummy, yummy! Bye!

Table

Basket

Frog

Bed

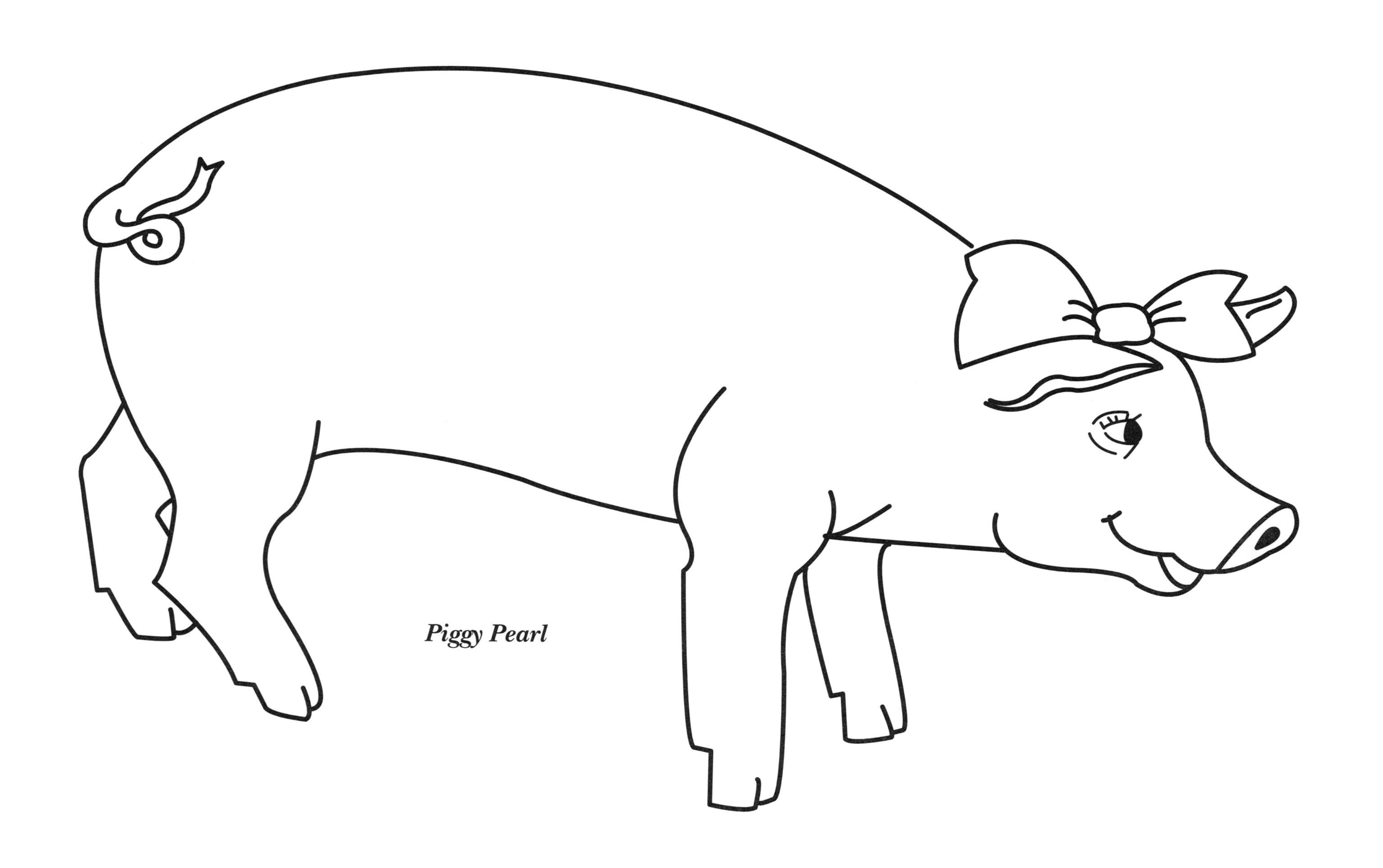
Piggy Pearl

Troll

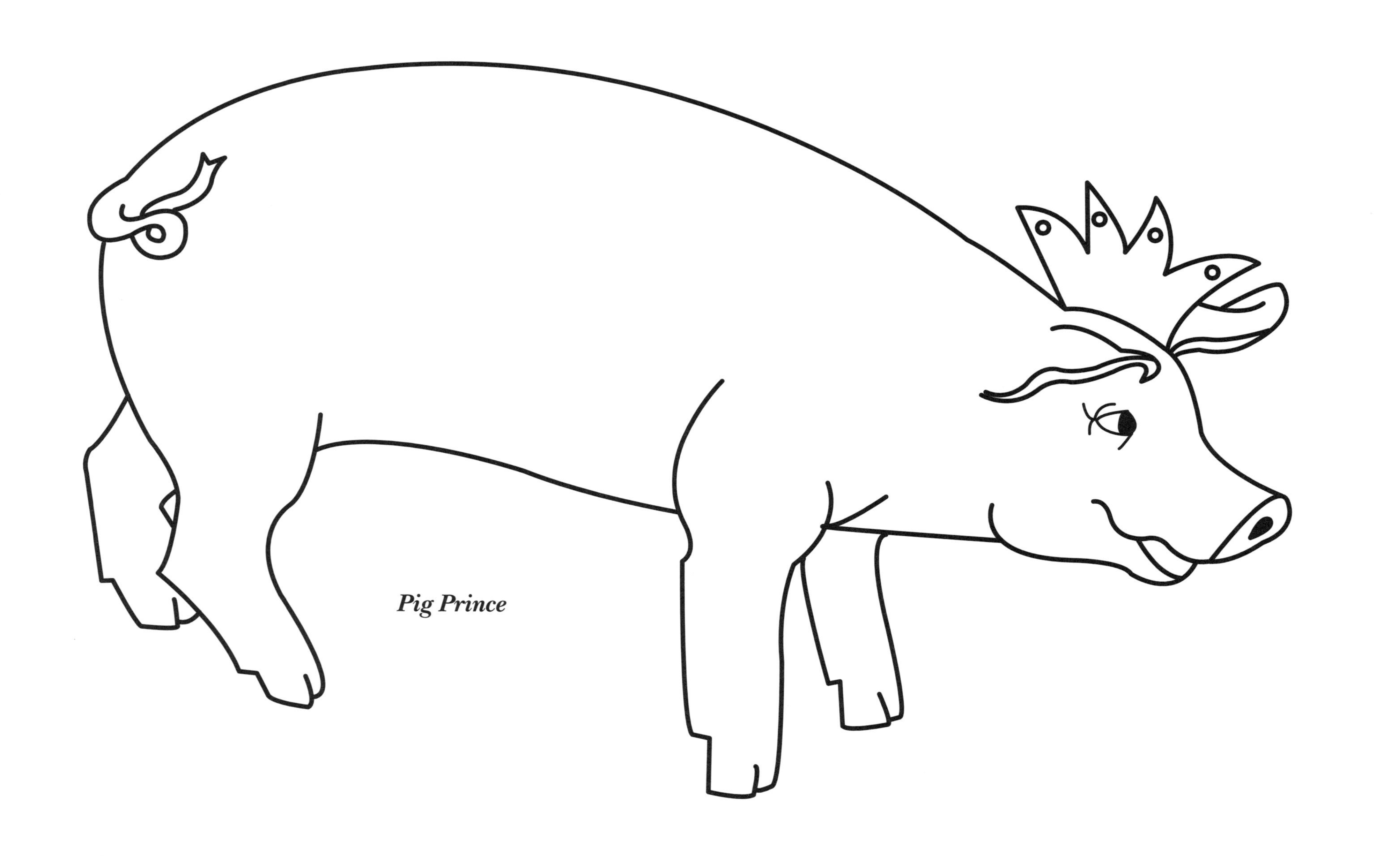
Pig Prince

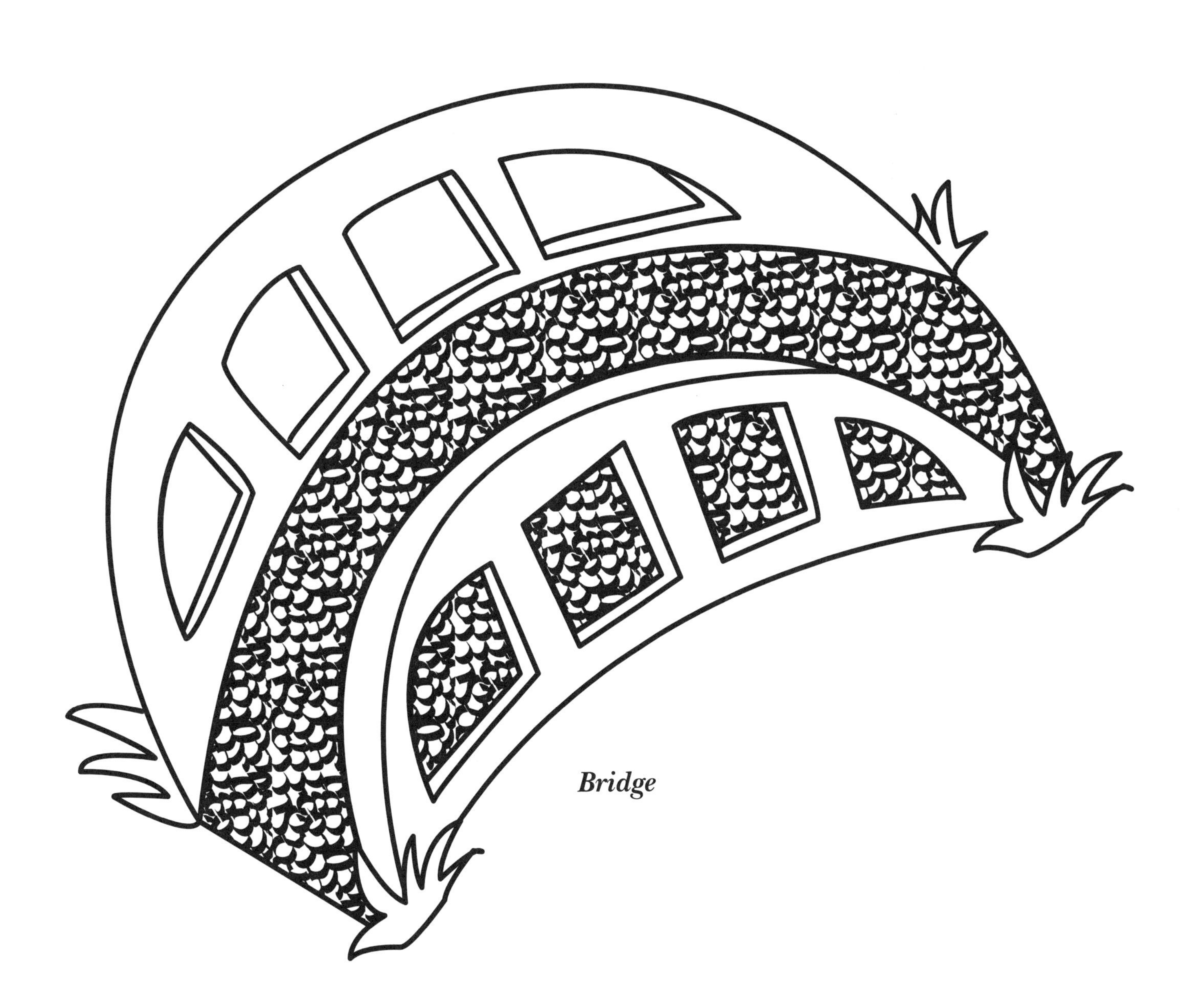

Bridge

Wolf

N is for TRINKA NOBLE

TRINKA HAKES NOBLE was born in Michigan, where she grew up on a farm and attended a one room school. Art was always an important part of her life, and following her graduation from Michigan State University she worked as an art teacher.

Ms. Noble is a versatile author who learned how to illustrate children's books from Uri Shulevitz. The first book that she both wrote and illustrated was *The King's Tea* (Dial, 1979). She also wrote and illustrated *Hansy's Mermaid* (Dial, 1983), which has realistic, beautiful paintings. She is best known, however, as the author of the very popular "Jimmy's Boa" stories illustrated by Stephen Kellogg.

She now lives in New Jersey with her husband.

Before Sharing Books

The boa in the Jimmy's Boa stories is a delightful fellow. Compare him to a real boa. These are warm climate, colorful reptiles from Mexico and Central America.

Boas eat meat, and catch their prey by wrapping their strong body around it and squeezing. Boas have a small horny claw on each side of their body. This is a tiny hipbone! Compare the illustrations that Stephen Kellogg designed for *The Day Jimmy's Boa Ate the Wash* to those by Noble in her self-illustrated book *Hansy's Mermaid.* What do you think the Jimmy's boa would have looked like if Trinka Noble had done the pictures herself? Do you prefer the pictures of Noble or those of Kellogg?

Books to Share

The Day Jimmy's Boa Ate the Wash. Dial, 1980. It started out as an ordinary field trip to a farm, that is, until Jimmy's pet boa got loose.

Hansy's Mermaid. Dial, 1983. A storm brings a mermaid to a Dutch family, but Hansy, the young son, helps her return to the sea.

Jimmy's Boa Bounces Back. Dial, 1984. Jimmy's pet boa wreaks havoc at a posh garden party.

Meanwhile, Back at the Ranch. Puffin, 1982. Rancher Hicks is bored and looking for diversion in the town of sleepy gulch. Little does he know, exciting things are happening to his wife while he is gone.

Warm-Up Activities

Chant

This is the Way the Boa Slides (To the tune of "This is the Way We Wash Our Clothes").

Use with *The Day Jimmy's Boa Ate the Wash* and *Jimmy's Boa Bounces Back.*

This is the way the boa slides, boa slides,
Boa slides.
This is the way the boa slides
So early in the morning.

Repeat with "Boa climbs," "Boa circles," and "Boa squeezes."

Action Rhyme

Snake

With diamonds in his eyes
(Make diamond with hands)
He slithers under summer skies.
(Make sun by circling arms over head)
Drawing a green line in the grass,
(Draw a squiggly line in the air with finger)
He makes me jump when I pass!
(Jump on the word "jump")

Follow-Up Activity

Poetry

Write a concrete poem about a boa constrictor. A concrete poem is a poem in which the words form the shape of the subject of the poem.

Or, write a clerihew about Jimmy's boa. A clerihew is a short poem consisting of two couplets, it is always about a famous person, whose name forms a line. The first and second line rhyme, as do the third and fourth. Start off by making a list of words that rhyme with "boa" and create your clerihew from there. Below is a sample.

Jimmy's Boa
Where did he go-a
He ate the wash on the farm
And cause lots of harm!

O is for JOANNE OPPENHEIM

JOANNE OPPENHEIM was born May 11, 1934, in Middletown, New Jersey. She has been writing children's books for a long time. Her husband is a lawyer, and she is an editor at the Bank Street College Media Group. She has three children who are now grown—James, Anthony and Stephanie. Joanne Oppenheim also likes to perform in plays in her local community theater. Ms. Oppenheim is co-author of *Choosing Books for Kids*

Before Sharing Books

Discuss rhyme and how it is used in the text of Ms. Oppenheim's books.

Rhyme is the repeated words at the end of a sentence or phrase that sound alike. It is very important to the flow of Ms. Oppenheim's stories, especially *"Not Now," Said the Cow* and *"Uh-Oh," Said the Crow.*

Books to Share

Do You Like Cats? Bantam Little Rooster, 1993. Simple rhymed texts presents different kinds of cats and their behavior.

Left and Right. Gulliver Books, 1989. Two brothers, Left and Right, must stop bickering and learn to collaborate if they are to be successful cobblers.

Mrs. Peloki's Class Play. Dodd Mead, 1984. The dress rehearsal of Cinderella is a disaster, but the performance has a surprise ending.

"Not Now," Said the Cow. Bantam, 1989. In this story, based on the *Little Red Hen*, a black crow asks his animal friends to help him plant corn.

The Story Book Prince. Gulliver Books, 1987. It's bedtime, but this small prince outlasts them all until a clever old woman comes up with the perfect solution: a bedtime story!

"Uh-Oh," Said the Crow. Bantam, 1993. On a dark and windy night the animals in the barn are frightened by strange noises they think might be a ghost.

Warm-Up Activity

Chant

Donkey's Chant

Clip, clop, clip, clop
And they went on their way
Clip, clop, clip, clop
On that very hot day.
Clip, clop, clip, clop.

Have children chant in appropriate places during the telling of *The Donkey's Tale.*

Follow-Up Activity

"Not Now," Said the Cow Reader's Theater. Assign the parts of crow, cow, sheep, chick, donkey, rabbit, hog, cat, and mare to a child or group of children. Give them each a copy of the patterns to make stick puppets or a poster for a group. Recite the story with each child or group chiming in at the appropriate place. It helps to write the words on the back of the appropriate poster or mask.

"Not Now," Said the Cow Patterns

Donkey
Pig
Sheep

"Not Now," Said the Cow Patterns

P is for PATRICIA POLACCO

PATRICIA POLACCO was born in Lansing, Michigan, to an artistic family of Russian extraction. She studied art in the US and Australia, where she earned Bachelor's and Master's degrees in art, and a Doctorate in art history.

Ms. Polacco says that when she writes stories, she likes rocking in one of her thirteen rocking chairs, while picturing the ideas and hearing the words in her head. The stories she creates are based on her own experiences with her family. *The Keeping Quilt*, for instance, is about a real quilt her family used for special occasions.

She lives with her husband Enzo, and children,Traci and Steven in Oakland, California. Ms. Polacco also enjoys running, sculpting, painting and making Ukrainian eggs.

Before Sharing Books

In the Ukraine, there is a beautiful folk art called pysanky, which is the decorating of eggs. A small writing instrument called a kistka is used to draw on the eggs with beeswax and dye. The eggs take many hours to complete, and the finished work is very intricate, as well as beautiful.

The designs are based on traditional symbols that represent important real and spiritual events and ideals—wheat means a bountiful harvest, waves of ribbons mean eternity. The colors are also symbolic—pink for success, blue for health. The eggs are a popular form of art and are displayed all year round.

Patricia Polacco has included the colors, symbols and designs of pysanky in her books; they are central to the story in *Rechenka's Eggs*. Look for these eggs and designs in her other stories.

Books to Share

Babushka's Doll. Simon and Schuster, 1990. A little girl gets a doll that is twice as rambunctious as she is.

Chicken Sunday. Philomel, 1992. To thank Miss Eula for her fine Sunday chicken dinners, three children sell eggs to get money to buy her an Easter bonnet.

Rechenka's Eggs. Philomel, 1988. An injured goose breaks the painted eggs intended for the Easter Festival, but then replaces them with 13 beautiful eggs of her own.

Uncle Vova's Tree. Philomel, 1989. A whole family gathers at a farmhouse to celebrate Christmas in the Russian tradition.

Warm-Up Activities

Chant

Odin, Dva, Tri [One, Two, Three]

Odin (ah-DEEN), dva (DVAH),
tri, (TREE)!
Pazhahlsta (pah-ZHAH-luh-sta),
yayetsa (yah-yee-seh-AW)
depeya (deh-pek-YAH)
emyenya (EM-yehen-ya).
Odin, Babushka (BAH-bush-kah)
Odin, Brat (BRAHT)
Odin, Sestra (syeh-STRAH)
Odin, dva, tri!
Yayetsa depeya emyenya!

1, 2, 3!
Please, eggs for me.
One, Grandmother,
One brother, one sister,
1, 2, 3,
Eggs for me!

Action Rhyme

Karavai (A traditional Soviet rhyme)

(Hold hands in a circle)

We have a round loaf
(raise joined hands overhead)
So high
So high
(Stoop down)
So low
So low
(make circle as large as possible)
So wide
So wide
(move in together towards the center)
So narrow
So narrow.
(move back to regular-size circle)
Round loaf, round loaf, let he who wishes take some.
(One child moves to the center, then takes someone else's place, on the side of the circle. Begin the rhyme again.)

Follow-Up Activity

Mock Pysanky

Materials: Eggs, white wax crayons, food coloring, saucepan, water, stove.

Directions: Draw pattern on an unboiled egg with the wax crayon, being careful not to press too hard. Put a few drops of food coloring and the water into the saucepan and hard boil the egg. Let the egg cool. The food coloring will color the egg in the places where there is no wax.

Additional Selected Books by Patricia Polacco

The Bee Tree. Putnam and Grossett, 1993. In order to teach the value of books, a father leads his daughter and a growing crowd to a bee hive.

The Keeping Quilt. Simon and Schuster, 1988. A homemade quilt ties together the lives of four generations of an immigrant Jewish family.

Some Birthday. Simon and Schuster, 1991. A father takes his daughter to see a monster on her birthday.

Thunder Cake. Putnam and Grossett, 1993. Grandmother finds an unusual way to dispel her grandchild's fear of thunder.

Tikvahmeans. Doubleday, 1994. After a fire, a Jewish family finds symbols of hope among the ashes.

Q *is for PATRICIA QUINLAN*

PATRICIA QUINLAN has enjoyed expressing herself through writing since she was a child. Reading stories to her nieces and nephews inspired her to write books for kids. She says, "Writing keeps me in touch with the child in me." Ms. Quinlan was born and raised in Toronto, Canada, where she still lives. She has a bachelor's degree in philosophy and a master's degree in education from the University of Toronto. She likes to write and also gives workshops on writing for school children. She also writes stories in response to questions she has been asked by children she knows. For example, *Planting Seeds* was written about war fears for a neighbor's child.

Before Sharing Books

Ms. Quinlan is an author whose work is important because of the issues she chooses to address. It is very difficult to write about death and disease in an informative, realistic, yet sensitive manner. Try discussing some of the subjects Ms. Quinlan has chosen: AIDS and death, unemployment, and war. What other topics are the children concerned about? Have the group write a letter to Ms. Quinlan asking her to write a book about an area of particular concern to them.

Books to Share

Anna's Red Sled. Firefly, 1989. An old red sled holds memories and wishes from childhood for Anna and her mother.

Emma's Sea Journey. Firefly, 1991. Emma's imaginings lead her on a journey away from Glace Bay, her home, to a tropical island and under the sea.

My Dad Takes Care of Me. Firefly, 1987. A young boy's father loses his factory job. Both the boy and the father feel sad about it, but then they realize that taking care of each other is an important job also.

Planting Seeds. Firefly, 1988. This book addresses the psychological fears children have about nuclear war, as well as the ways people can resolve conflicts peacefully. Includes a bibliography of books to promote further discussion on these topics.

Tiger Flowers. Dial, 1994. When his Uncle Michael dies of AIDS, Joel's dreams and thoughts of him become a way of keeping his memory alive. A very sensitive and compassionate book.

Warm-Up Activities

Chant

Helping Dad (Use with My Dad Takes Care of Me)

This is the way I pound a nail
When I'm helping my Dad.
And when he sees how hard I worked
He smiles and he is glad.

(Repeat with various actions such as make my bed, rake the lawn, etc.)

Action Rhyme

How to Make a Happy Day

Two eyes to see nice things to do,
Two lips to smile the whole day through,
Two ears to hear what others say,
Two hands to put my things away.

A tongue to speak sweet words today,
A love filled heart for work or play.
Two feet that to you gladly run
To happy days for everyone.

(Follow directions in verse)

Follow-Up Activity

Writing Activity

Write a group story about a common childhood experience, such as feelings, being sick, or remembering special things.

Begin by having the children brainstorm a list of experiences that you record on a poster board or in some way for the whole group to see. Then have the children select a favorite.

Write the chosen experience at the top of a new sheet, and have the group list the sights, sounds, and actions that make up this experience.

Compose a story using the list you made.

R *is for FAITH RINGGOLD*

FAITH RINGGOLD is an African American author and artist. She was born in Harlem in 1930, and still lives there half the year. The other half of the year, she is a professor of fine art and the University of California at San Diego.

Ms. Ringgold's artwork has focused on African American women, and her children's books, having grown from her art, have also had that focus. *Tar Beach*, one of Ms. Ringgold most well-loved stories, was written in 1988 on a painted "story quilt" of the same name. The original quilt is now hanging in the Guggenheim Museum in New York City. Ms. Ringgold says that she started making her story quilts because she could not get her stories published. The quilts are very effective, as those who view them "see" the story also. Her quilts have easily made the format transition to children's books.

Before Sharing Books

Collect and display books about African American artists, such as *Faith Ringgold* by Robin Turner (Little Brown, 1993) and *Li'L Sis and Uncle Willy* by Gwen Everett (Smithsonian Institute, 1991). Show examples of native African art also. Compare these to the pictures by Faith Ringgold. What might have influenced Ms. Ringgold's style? Are there influences from native African art or other African American artists in her work?

Books to Share

Aunt Harriet's Underground Railroad in the Sky. Crown, 1993. The story of Harriet Tubman and the Underground Railroad is brought to life through the fantastic adventure of Cassie and Bebe Lightfoot and their magical flights.

Dinner at Aunt Connie's House. Hyperion, 1993. For Melody, the best part of summer is visiting Aunt Connie at her big, beautiful house by the sea. The attic is full of surprises this summer, painted by Aunt Connie herself.

Tar Beach. Crown, 1992. *Tar Beach* is the book that was based on a story quilt. Cassie Lightfoot takes an imaginary journey, flying with the George Washington Bridge as a necklace. Cassie and her brother Bebe have many adventures in the sky.

Warm-Up Activities

Chant

(To use with Tar Beach).

Be a busy quilter
Sew and paint all day.
When your quilt is finished
Tell a story that way.

When night comes
Fly though the sky.
A magic quilted story
My, so high.

Follow-Up Activities

Writing Activity

Choose some biographies of famous African Americans to share with the children. Have them draw pictures or write a paragraph on colored construction paper. Make a border around the edge of each with scraps of wrapping paper. Tape these all together to form a story quilt.

S is for ALLEN SAY

ALLEN SAY was born in Yokohama, Japan, in 1937. He dreamed of becoming a cartoonist from the age of six, and at age twelve, apprenticed himself to his favorite cartoonist, Noro Shinpei. For the next four years, Say learned to draw and paint under the direction of Noro, who has remained Say's mentor. Say illustrated his first children's book—published in 1972—in a photo studio between shooting assignments. For years after this first book, he continued writing and illustrating children's books on a part-time basis.

In 1987, while illustrating *The Boy of the Three Year Nap*, he decided to commit himself full time to writing and illustrating his beloved books. Since then, he has written and illustrated six books, including *Grandfather's Journey*, winner of the 1994 Caldecott medal. His books usually have a Japanese setting and the characters often convey messages of coexistence and relationships. Many of his stories are autobiographical, such as *Grandfather's Journey* and *The Ink-Keeper's Apprentice*.

Before Sharing Books

Allen Say was an apprentice to a famous cartoonist. Compare and contrast Say's illustrations to the cartoon-type illustrations of Tomi Ungerer or the flat, colorful pictures of Donald Crews. Discuss the differences between cartoon or comic illustration and the form of watercolors used in Allen Say's books. Why does your group think Mr. Say chose to become an illustrator instead of a cartoonist?

Books to Share

The Bicycle Man. Houghton Mifflin, 1982. Two American soldiers perform amazing tricks on a borrowed bicycle in occupied Japan. A Reading Rainbow book.

El Chino. Houghton Mifflin, 1990. The true story of Billy Wong, the first Chinese bullfighter.

Grandfather's Journey. Houghton Mifflin, 1993. Allan Say gives a poignant account of his family's cross cultural experiences through reminiscences of his grandfather's life in Japan and America. Winner of the 1994 Caldecott Medal.

The Ink-Keeper's Apprentice. Houghton Mifflin, 1994. Tells the story of a twelve-year-old boy on his own who apprentices himself to a famous cartoonist in Japan.

Tree of Cranes. Houghton Mifflin, 1991. A boy's first Christmas is made special when his mother surprises him with beautiful silver cranes while he is ill with a cold. ALA Notable book and BCCB Blue Ribbon winner.

Warm-Up Activities

Chant

Best Thing

(To use with The Ink-Keeper's Apprentice)

What thing can you do the best?
Help us so we can guess.
Can you draw or read a book?
Can you sing or can you cook?
Tell us now
Give us a clue
For we like you.

Action Rhyme

(To use with The Ink-Keeper's Apprentice)

Everyone has lots
Of feelings inside
And when you're nice to others
Those feelings won't hide

Feelings are special;
When they feel good to you—
And all of your friends
Have good feelings, too.

Follow-Up Activities

Writing Activity

Thank You Books

At the end of the story *The Bicycle Man*, the American soldiers say thank you to the Japanese people— "Ari-ga-tow." Research how to say thank you in several languages. Have each child copy the translations of "thank you" you choose and their English pronunciation on paper. They can then illustrate situations where "thank you" might be said in that country. Bind or staple together to make a Thank You book.

Additional Selected Books by Allen Say

The Lost Lake. Houghton Mifflin, 1989. Luke's father is upset that his favorite lake has been overrun by tourists, so he takes Luke on a long hike to find a new lake.

A River Dream. Houghton, 1988. A boy takes a fantasy fly fishing trip up a river with his uncle. A *New York Times* Best Children's Book.

T *is for KEIZABURO TEJIMA*

KEIZABURO TEJIMA was born in 1935 in Hokkaido, the northernmost island of Japan. He is a member of the Japanese Woodcut Society, and uses this bold traditional method in his books.

Some of the most unusually illustrated books have been done by Tejima in his woodcut style. Using beautiful two-page spreads and glossy inks, he creates pictures by gouging the designs out of a block of wood, then rubbing with ink to make a print. Nature settings are expressed breathtakingly through this interesting process.

Before Sharing Books

Woodcut is the method of illustration used by Tejima. Woodcuts are created when a design is drawn on soft wood and is then carved out using special tools. The design is then covered with ink, and a piece of rice paper is placed over it. The paper is burnished or pressed, and then lifted off. Tejima uses the traditional Japanese version of this art.

Books to Share

Bear's Autumn. Simon and Schuster, 1986. Set in the mountains of Hokkaido, Japan, this tells the story of the real and imaginary fall activities of a mother bear and her cub.

Fox's Dream. Putnam, 1987. *New York Times* Best Illustrated Children's Book. While wandering through the winter forest, a lonely fox has an enchanting vision, and then is lonely no longer.

Ho-Lim Lim: A Rabbit Tale from Japan. Putnam, 1990. After one last foray for food, an old rabbit decides it is better to let his grandchildren bring him food by the fire.

Owl Lake. Philomel, 1987. As the sun slips down behind the lake and the sky darkens, Father Owl comes out and hunts for fish to feed his hungry family.

Swan Sky. Philomel, 1988. Despite the attentions of her family, a young swan is unable to make the flight to their summertime home.

Warm-Up Activities

Chant

Ho-Lim Lim

Yukara song of the Ainu
Rabbit called Isopo kamuy
Jump, Isopo Kamuy
Jump high to the sky—
Though gulls were men
Though weeds were whales
Though clouds were smoke.
Nap now while children feed you.

Follow-Up Activity

Movement Activities

Share the book *Bear's Autumn.* Have the children act out the movements of the mother bear and her cub—eating grapes, climbing a tree, fishing for salmon, swimming, and playing in the river.

Styrofoam Block Prints

Materials: Styrofoam packaging from meat or fruit and a nail to use for drawing.

Directions: Children can use a nail to gouge a drawing onto the styrofoam package. Then, using tempra paints, paint the surface of the styrofoam, being careful not to let the paint fill in the lines of the design. Place a piece of construction paper on the inked surface and rub over the back with a plastic spoon. Lift off the paper carefully after testing a corner. The design will appear as white against a painted background.

U *is for TOMI UNGERER*

TOMI UNGERER was born in France on November 28, 1931. Beginning his career as a cartoonist, Mr. Ungerer translated his editorial cartoon style and ideas over into his children's books. Today, he creates popular children's picture books full of satire and social comment. *Crictor, Emile* and *The Hat* are good examples of this characteristic in Ungerer's work. Although good seems to always triumph over evil in his stories, he has a somewhat unusual view of those two concepts.

Unusual words and phrases also appeal to this author. Throughout his books, words such as "blunderbuss" and "tilbury" can be found. These words may not be part of the vocabulary of the intended audience, but they play upon a child's delight of repeating melodious, mysterious phrases. Ungerer credits his love of language to his mother, who "taught him how to imagine." He also looked at the artistic works of Mathias Gruenwald and Albrecht Durer for artistic inspiration.

Before Sharing Books

Many of the stories by Tomi Ungerer feature unusual animals as heros. In *Rufus,* the hero is a bat; in *Emile,* an octopus; and in *Crictor,* a snake. Have the children help you think of other books with unusual animals heros. (Examples: *Stellaluna* by Janell Canon, Harcourt Brace Jovanovich, 1993; *The Armadillo from Amarillo* by Lynn Cherry, Harcourt Brace Jovanovich, 1994). Even Ungerer's human characters are unusual—an ogre, three robbers, etc. Why does your group think Mr. Ungerer chooses unusual animals and humans?

Books to Share

Adelaide. Dell, 1991. Adelaide's parents are surprised when they see their new baby kangaroo has wings. Soon, Adelaide leaves home to travel the world, have adventures, get married, and become a heroine.

Crictor. HarperCollins, 1958. Crictor, a friendly snake, saves his mistress from various kinds of trouble.

Emile. Dell, 1992. Emile the Octopus rescues Captain Samofar and becomes a hero.

Rufus. Dell, 1991. Rufus the bat tries life in the daylight, but prefers to hunt moths at night for his friend Dr. Tarturo.

Warm-Up Activities

Chant

I'm glad I'm not
An octopus, boa, or bat
But these three, I'm sure would agree
Wouldn't want to be me!

Action Rhyme

Here is Crictor on the ground
(Wiggle arm)
Wrapping around what he's found.
(Wrap arms around self)
Here is Rufus, flying up high
(Flap arms)
Spreading wings on the night sky.
(Spread arms out)
Here is the Emile, do you see?
(Wiggle fingers)
Swimming gently under the sea.

Follow-Up Activities

Puppet show *Octorella* starts on p. 63.

Additional Selected Books by Tomi Ungerer

Beast of M. Racine, Farrar, Straus, and Giroux, 1971. A pair of clever children fool everyone into believing they are a strange beast.

Three Robbers. Macmillan, 1987. Three fierce robbers terrify the countryside until they are charmed by a little girl named Tiffany.

Zelda's Ogre. Delacorte, 1991. A mean giant ogre likes to eat only tender young children until Zelda dazzles his taste buds with her culinary skills.

Octorella

The show takes place underwater and the heroine is one of Tomi Ungerer's unusual animals: an octopus!

Characters:

Octorella (Octopus)
Sister Crusty (Crab)
Sister Wiggles (Jelly Fish)
Mother Shrimpy (Shrimp)
Fairy Codmother (Fish)
Prince Eightarms (Octopus)

Octorella is sweeping and humming. Sister Crusty enters

CRUSTY: Octorella! Aren't you finished bottom sweeping yet. You still need to untangle the seaweed garden and make some clam chowder for dinner. And I want you to sharpen my claws before I get my beauty rest. Hurry up!

OCTORELLA: I'm sorry Sister Crusty dear. I'm just so tired and hungry. Could you help me a little, please?

CRUSTY: What?? Are you crazy?? I'm not a bottom sweeper, and I don't do seaweed. Besides, if I help you I wont have time to put my new mud pack beauty treatment on.

(Sister Wiggles enters)

SISTER WIGGLES: Octorella! I'm waiting for you to braid my tentacles. Hurry up with that sweeping. And another thing, I'm hungry. Where's my clam chowder??

OCTORELLA: I'm sorry, Sister Wiggles. I'm hurrying.

SISTER WIGGLES: Well, hurry faster!

(Mother Shrimpy enters)

MOTHER SHRIMPY: Girls, girls! Oh, my beautiful sea urchins, I have wonderful news. Prince Eightarms is having an underwater ball at the Coral Palace tonight, and we are invited!

SISTER WIGGLES: A ball! What fun. Now, hurry it up, Octorella. You must help me dress for the ball so I can meet Prince Eightarms.

SISTER CRUSTY: Yeah, Octorella, you must help me fix my hair so I can meet Prince Eightarms also.

OCTORELLA: Can I go to the ball??

CRUSTY: You?? Why you are all dirty tattered and torn.

WIGGLES: Yeah! We don't want you to go—we would be embarrassed. Besides, you don't have anything to wear.

MOTHER SHRIMPY: No, Octorella, a ball is no place for you. You will stay home and polish all the pearls in our collection. Crabby, Wiggles, hurry along now and get ready for the ball.

(Shrimpy, Wiggles, and Crabby exit.)

OCTORELLA: Oh! I wish I could go to the ball. Prince Eightarms is so handsome. *(Sigh!)*

FAIRY CODMOTHER: My, my, I thought I heard a wish in the water, and here you are, Octorella.

OCTORELLA: Who are you? Where did you come from and how do you know my name??

FAIRY CODMOTHER: I'm your Fairy Codmother, and I have come to answer your wish.

OCTORELLA: Oh, my! I didn't even know I had a Fairy Codmother. But can you help me? I was wishing to go to the ball at the Coral Palace and meet Prince Eightarms.

FAIRY CODMOTHER: I think that can be arranged.

OCTORELLA: But look at me—I'm a mess and I have nothing to wear.

FAIRY CODMOTHER: I will take care of that, two. Bring me 10 pearls from your pearl collection.

(Octorella exits and returns)

OCTORELLA: Here they are.

FAIRY CODMOTHER: Good. Stand back while I do some magic. Bubbly sea form, coral bright, get Octorella to the ball tonight!

OCTORELLA: Why, look! the pearls have turned into a beautiful ball gown and a trusty seahorse. And look, one, two, three, four, five, six, seven, eight lovely mother-of-pearl slippers that fit perfectly on my eight octopus feet! Oh, thank you Fairy Codmother.

FAIRY CODMOTHER: No trouble at all. Just be back before the last air bubble busts at midnight. If you are not, your dress and shoes will turn back into pearls.

OCTORELLA: I will! Goodbye!

FAIRY CODMOTHER: Have fun, child! *(Exits)*

SCENE TWO

(Octorella enters the ball)

OCTORELLA: I can't believe I'm here at the ball. Look, there's Crusty and Wiggles. And there is Prince Eightarms. He is so handsome. Wait... he's coming this way!

PRINCE EIGHTARMS: Hello there. May I have this dance with you, my lovely Octopus??

OCTORELLA: Certainly, Prince Eightarms.

(They begin dancing and laughing. Bubbles begin to pop. After the twelfth one) ...

OCTORELLA: Oh no! The last air bubble! I must go. Goodbye!! *(Runs out)*

PRINCE EIGHTARMS: Wait! I don't even know your name. Oh, she's gone. What's this. It's one of her mother-of-pearl slippers...and here's another, and another. Eight! Eight mother-of-pearl slippers! I will not rest until I find the eight dainty feet that fit these slipper!

SCENE THREE

OCTORELLA: I'm so glad I got to go to the ball. Prince Eightarms was so nice and charming.

(Crabby and Wiggles enter)

CRABBY: Ho, Octorella. Did you miss a fun party.

WIGGLES: Yeah, it was great, in spite of the fact that Prince Eightarms danced all night with some octopus. She ran out at midnight and didn't even take her shoes!

SHRIMPY: Yes, and now the Prince is determined to marry the one whose feet fit the shoes.

(A loud knock at the door and announcement "Make way for Prince Eightarms!")

PRINCE EIGHTARMS: Hello ladies. I'm searching for a special girl, one whose beautiful feet fit these eight dainty slippers. Would you like to try??

CRABBY: Me first, me first. I have eight legs.

PRINCE EIGHTARMS: Uuuuugh! These dainty shoes won't fit on your pointy hard feet. You are not the one. Who's next to try on the shoes??

WIGGLES: Me, me me! My feet aren't pointy—try me!

PRINCE EIGHTARMS: Ohhhh! your feet are all soft and squishy—like jelly. These shoes keep sliding off! You are not the one either! Anyone else??

CRABBY AND WIGGLES: NO!

OCTORELLA: How about me??

CRABBY AND WIGGLES: You Octorella??? Ha, ha, ha! She thinks the prince might want to marry her!

PRINCE EIGHTARMS: Silence! Come my dear, try these shoes. My, but you do have dainty feet. And look, the first shoe fits. And the second and third, fourth, fifth, sixth, seventh, and eighth. It is you, my lovely octopus. Please marry me!

OCTORELLA: I will, I will! Goodbye sisters!! (Octorella and Prince exit.)

WIGGLES: Humpf! I guess they will live happily ever after.

CRABBY: Yeah, as happy as you can be when you have eight legs!

THE END

Fairy Codmother

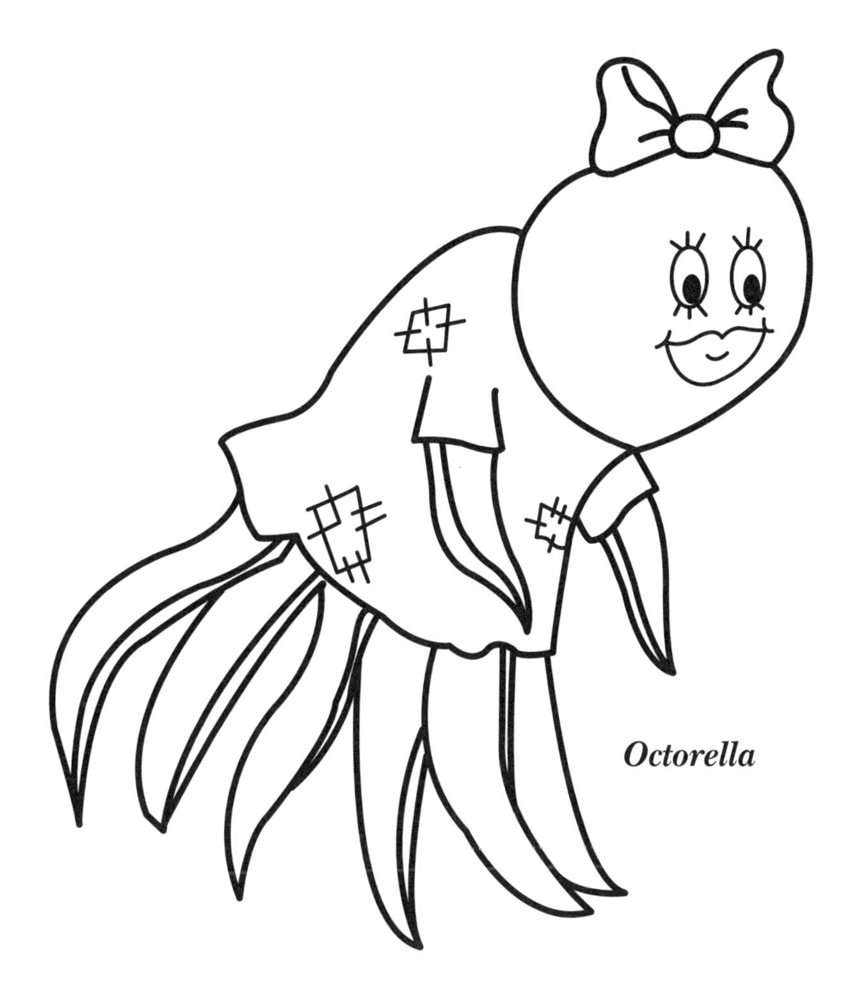

Octorella

Crusty

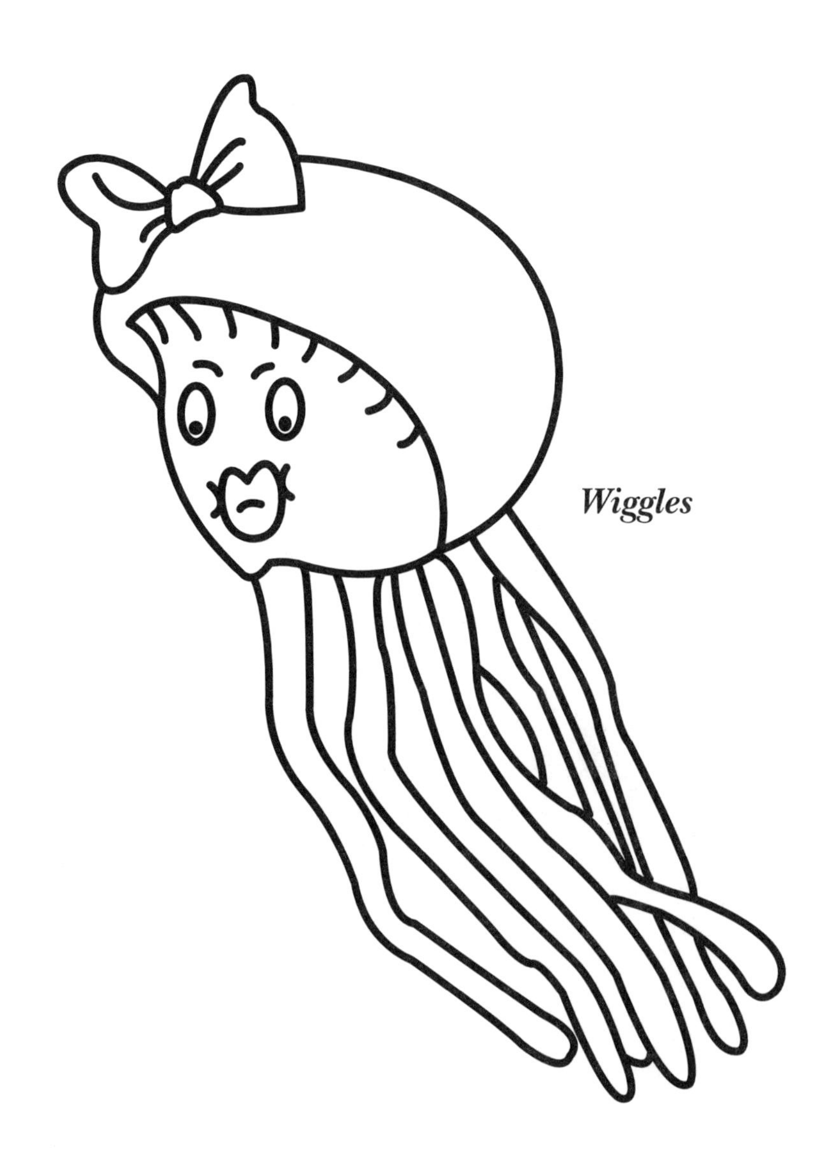

Wiggles

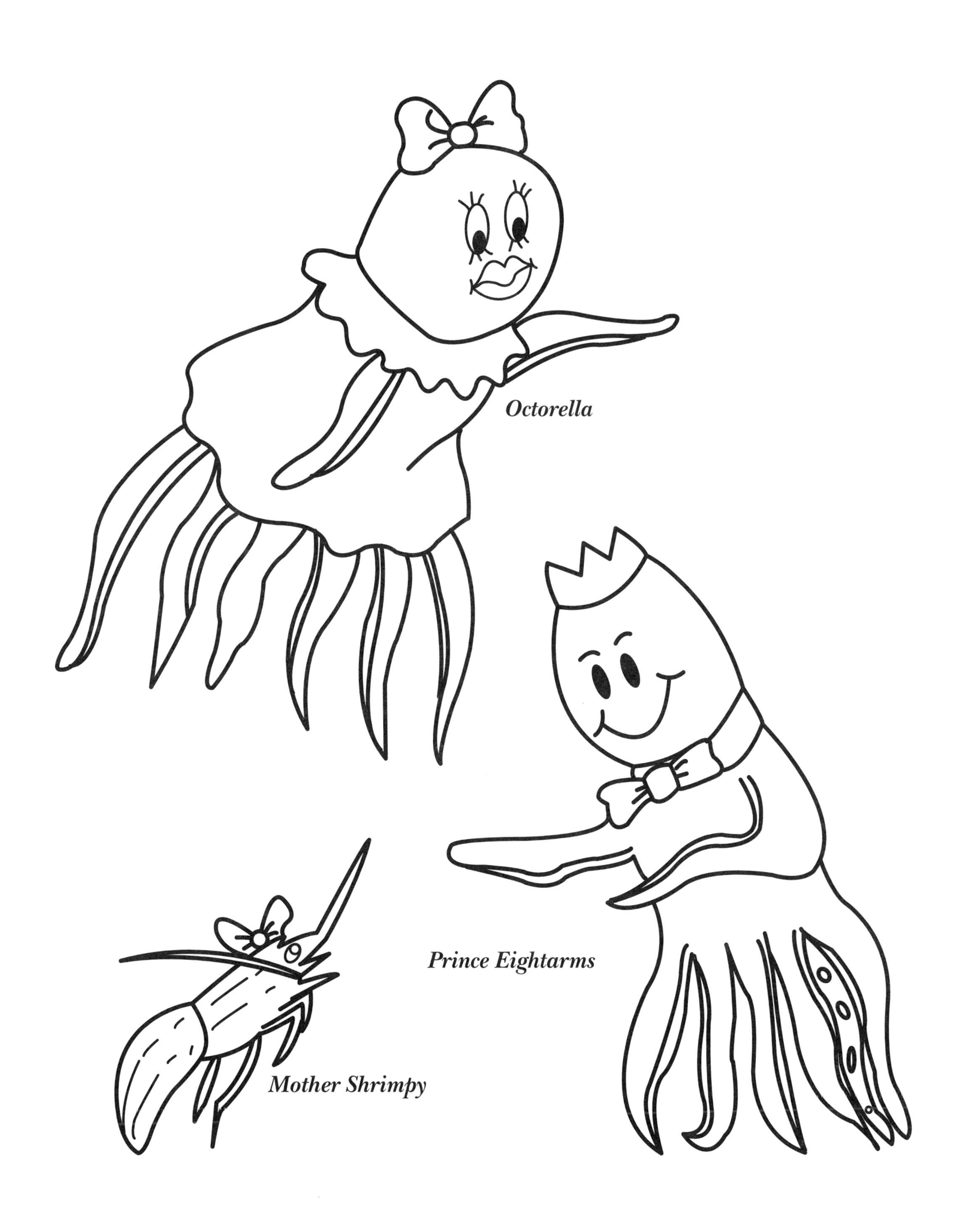
Octorella
Prince Eightarms
Mother Shrimpy

V *is for NANCY VAN LAAN*

NANCY VAN LAAN was born in Baton Rouge, Louisiana, in 1939. Her father was an Air Force colonel, and her family moved often as she was growing up. She attended schools in Canada, England, and the United States.

When Ms. Van Laan was just seventeen, she started her own dance company, and then choreographed "The Wizard of Oz" into a ballet that was shown on the Alabama Educational Television Network, where it won a special production award. Ms. Van Laan was planning a career in dance,which was ended abruptly when she broke the base of her spine in a sledding accident. She then decided to pursue a degree in Radio/TV at the University of Alabama. This led to a job as a censor at ABC-TV. She continued her studies in drama at Rutgers University and received a MFA in theater. After that, Ms. Van Laan authored two plays that received awards for regional theater. In 1989, she started writing full time. She likes to be very busy and always has lots going on, even when she writes. "Writing is a part of me..." says Van Laan, "Not writing makes me grumpy, restless, bored, anxious, lackadaisical, and in short, miserable. So I write."

Before Sharing Books

Ms. Van Laan has created a selection of varied and lively works that reflect both her theater and dance training. *Possum Come A-Knockin* is in the form of a rollicking rhyme, and *Rainbow Crow* contains chants that remind us of those of a formal chorus in classical theater. Her other stories inevitably contain repeated phrases for joining in and speaking out loud. You might try to find other stories that work well for group reading from the authors included in this book. Start with *"Not Now" Said the Cow* by Joanne Oppenheim and *Peanut Butter and Jelly* by Nadine Westcott.

Books to Share

The Big, Fat Worm. Knopf, 1987. An uncomplicated tale about a worm featuring repeated phrases that encourage group participation.

The Legend of El Dorado. Knopf, 1991. The powerful legend of the man who would sacrifice anything to learn the forbidden secrets of the South American jungle.

Possum Come A-Knockin. Knopf, 1990. A possum plays mischievous pranks on a whole family. Text told in rhythm and rhyme. *School Library Journal* Starred Book.

A Mouse in My House. Knopf, 1990. A small boy imagines that he sees himself in everything from a small bug to a bumbling bear. *School Library Journal* Starred Book.

Rainbow Crow. Knopf, 1989. Tells the story of how Rainbow Crow loses his sweet voice and brilliant colors to bring fire and life to the woodland animals, who are perishing in a blizzard. A Reading Rainbow Book, Pennsylvania Children's Book Award.

Warm-Up Activities

Chant

For The Legend of El Dorado

Lake of sadness, full of gold
Now your legend must be told
Of the moon who made a lake
And the family it did take.
Chi-cha, chi-cha, chi-cha, chi-cha.

Rhyme

Rainbow Crow

Aiya, aiya, aiya, aiya.
Rain, Rainbow Crow,
Stop the snow, crow.
Fly to the sky high
Rain, Rainbow Crow.
Aiya, aiya, aiya, aiya.

Aiya, aiya, aiya, aiya.
Kind, young, brave crow
Saved us from the snow.
Flew to the sky high,
Brought back fire.
Now just plain crow
No more rainbow.
Aiya, aiya, aiya, aiya.

Follow-Up Activity

Drama

Use the book *Rainbow Crow* to put on a dramatic demonstration of the story. Children can play the parts of the different animals, the crow, and the sun. Teach them the Rainbow Crow chant included here.

Costumes for animals can be made from simple materials. Brown or black socks worn on both hands and feet make paws. Hooves can be made by tying back plastic flower pots on to hands and feet. Wings can be made by draping dress net over a child's shoulders. Stuffed socks, paper chains, and fringed cloth scraps make excellent tails. Make masks of animals by coloring and gluing fake fur to paper plates.

Perform for parents or other groups of children.

W *is for NADINE WESTCOTT*

NADINE BERNARD WESTCOTT had her first artistic success in the third grade when she won third place in a Cheerios coloring contest.

She pursued this early interest in art at Syracuse University, where she received a degree in fine arts. She worked as a designer and illustrator of greeting cards before she becoming a children's author. Ms. Wescott's illustrations are very humorous, much like the designs she created for the greeting card company. Her favorite type of book to illustrate has traditional stories, rhymes and songs.

She lives with her family in rural Woodstock, Vermont, where the countryside is much like that in the book *I Know an Old Lady Who Swallowed a Fly.*

Before Sharing Books

Discuss rhymes, chants, and songs, which Ms. Westcott uses as stories. Look at the book Anna Banana by Joanna Cole. Are there any other rhymes that would make good picture books? Also look at *This Old Man* by Robin Koontz (Dodd Mead, 1991) and *In a Cabin In a Wood* by Darcie McNally (Dutton, 1991).

Books to Share

The Lady With the Alligator Purse. Little Brown, 1988. A nonsense rhyme with pictures about Tiny Tim, who is sick but cured with pizza by the lady with the alligator purse.

Peanut Butter and Jelly. Puffin, 1993. Rhyming text and illustrations of this song explain how to make a peanut butter and jelly sandwich.

Skip to My Lou. Little Brown, 1992. When parents leave a young boy in charge of the farm one day, chaos erupts as the animals take over.

There's a Hole in the Bucket. Harper Collins, 1990. In this illustrated version of an old folk song, Liza instructs Henry how to fix a hole in the bucket, and Henry gives her all the reasons why he can't.

Warm-Up Activities

Chant

We sing a song

We sing a song
We lift our feet high and go,
We go along
We go along
We march and sing a song.

Follow-Up Activities

Mary Had a Little Lamb Puppet Show
(Begins on the next page)

Additional Selected Books by Tomi Ungerer

The Giant Vegetable Garden. Little Brown, 1981. In their desire to win the prize for the finest vegetables at the fair, the townspeople let their gardens grow until the plants threaten to strangle the village.

The House That Jack Built. Little Brown, 1991. The traditional rhyme is brought to life through lively illustrations and clever flaps and action devices.

I Know an Old Lady Who Swallowed a Fly. Little Brown, 1980. A cumulative rhyme in which the solution is worse that the predicament when an old lady swallows a fly.

Mary Had a Little Lamb

Use this puppet show based on a traditional rhyme, to show how Ms. Wescott expands traditional rhymes and songs in her book.

Characters:

Lamb
Spider
(See patterns to make stick puppets if needed.)

(Lamb enters)

LAMB: *(Crying)* Baaaaa! Baaaa! Baaaa!

SPIDER: (Drops down on string) Stop that! You are too noisy! You are hurting my sensitive spider ears. What's all the fuss about, anyway?

LAMB: EEEEEEEKK! (Runs away)

SPIDER: Come back, lamb!

LAMB: I'm sorry, I didn't mean to run. You scared me.

SPIDER: Don't worry, little lamb. I won't hurt you. What's wrong? Why are you crying so loudly?

LAMB: (Crying again) Baaaa! Baaaa! I lost my girl. I can't find her anywhere.

SPIDER: Girl? Oh, my!! I hope her name is not Miss Muffet. Are you looking for Miss Muffet??

LAMB: No, no. Baaaa! I'm looking for Mary.

SPIDER: Whew! Oh, boy is that a relief! I'm glad you are not looking for Miss Muffet.

LAMB: Why???

SPIDER: Because. I frightened Miss Muffet away. All I did was sit down beside her, and off she ran. (crying now, too) Boo, hoo, hoo! No one likes me, everybody hates me, I think I'll go eat flies! Oh, why does everyone think I'm ugly and scary??

LAMB: Oh, Spider! Don't feel so bad! Don't be so sad! Look at me. (Moves closer to spider) See, I'm not afraid of you. I'm not running away. And I don't even think you are ugly.

SPIDER: You…you don't?

LAMB: No, not at all, and you, uhhhh, have ahhhh, beautiful eyes, yeah, that's it, beautiful eyes.

SPIDER: Do you really think so?? Are you sure you are not just saying that to make me feel better?

LAMB: Why, no really, I mean it. Your eyes are nice and black and bright, and…and BEADY! I bet you can see so very well with those nice eyes. I bet you could even see Mary. *(crying again)* Oh, Mary, baaaa! Baaaa! *MARY!!* Come and find your little lamb with fleece as white as snow. *Baaaaaaaaa!!*

SPIDER: Awww, lamb, please don't cry. How about if I crawl to the very top of my web. I'll use my beady eyes to see her. What does she look like?

LAMB: Well, she is 6 years old and her two front teeth are missing. She has blonde curly hair with a big blue bow on top. She was wearing her favorite blue dress, and carrying a notebook, pencils, and a lunch sack.

SPIDER: It sounds like your Mary was on her way to school.

LAMB: Oh dear!!! Then I must go to school, because everywhere that Mary goes, I must surely go.

SPIDER: But you can't go to school.

LAMB: Why not??

SPIDER: Because, it's against the rules. It would make the children laugh and play to see a lamb in school. Mary would get in trouble and the teacher would send you out.

LAMB: Baaaa! Baaaaa! Baaaa!

SPIDER: Boy, you really do miss Mary a lot, don't you.

LAMB: Yes, I love her...and she loves me, too.

SPIDER: She loves you? Really?

LAMB: Yes.

SPIDER: Oh, I wish somebody loved me. But everyone is afraid of me.

LAMB: Spider?

SPIDER: Yes?

LAMB: I'm not afraid of you.

SPIDER: You're not?

LAMB: No. And Spider...

SPIDER: Yes?

LAMB: I love you!

SPIDER: You do? Really? Oh YIPPEE! I love you too, little lamb. You wait right here and I'll go to the top of my web and watch for Mary when the school bell rings. Thank you, thank you lamb.

LAMB: No, thank you, Spider. And tomorrow I'm going to have my Mary tell your Miss Muffet that you are BEAUTIFUL!

SPIDER: Yeah?

LAMB: Yeah!!

SPIDER: AND LAMB: *(To audience)* Isn't it nice to have someone to love?? Bye!!!

THE END

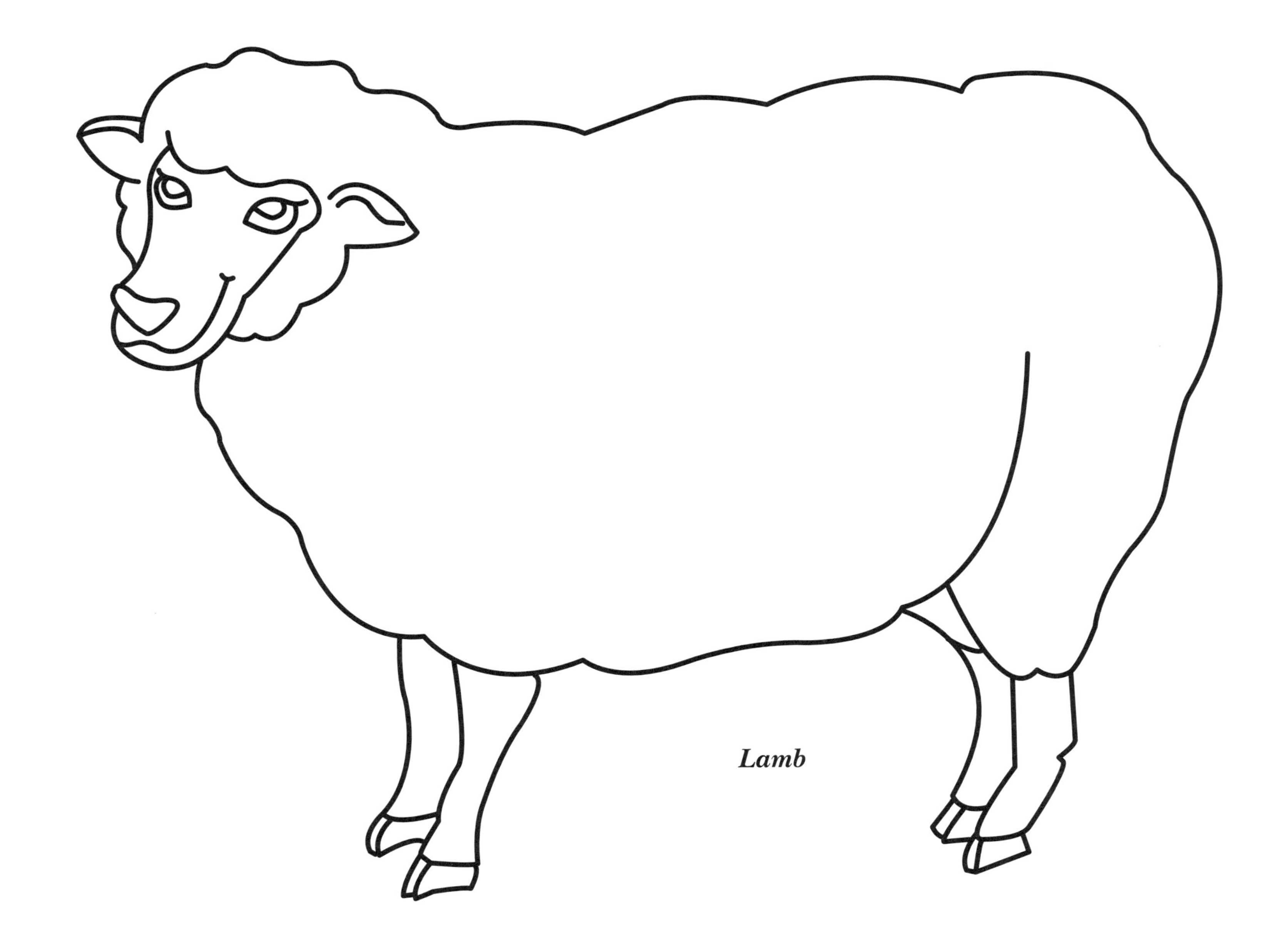

Lamb

Spider

VERNA AARDEMA was born June 6, 1911, in New Era, Michigan. Ms. Aardema was both a teacher and a journalist. An admitted bookworm, as a child she was always in a hurry to finish each chapter in a book, just so she could get started on the next one. She also liked to escape from chores by running out to the swamp behind her home, and it was there that she composed her first stories.

Although Ms. Aardema is not of African descent, she has determined through her writing to preserve African stories and oral traditions because of her fascination with the diversity found on the continent. To do so, she makes painstaking studies of culture and geography, and then writes modern adaptations of the stories of the time. The results are carefully crafted, authentic works that reflect different cultures accurately. Ms. Aardema uses magic, adventure and humor in her retellings, and often features animal heros who solve the mysteries of nature. Her book *Why Mosquitos Buzz in People's Ears* won the Caldecott Medal in 1976.

Before Sharing Books

Discuss the Masai people of Africa. The Masai people have no written history. Their past has been pieced together through legends and stories, such as *Who's In Rabbit's House?* Stories they tell often carry their traditions and beliefs in the story line. How does your group think Ms. Aardema did research for her stories that are from the Masai if they were not written down. Talk about oral history and how the children can record their family stories that are not written down.

Books to Share

Bringing the Rain to Kapiti Plain. Dial, 1981. A cumulative rhyming tale telling how Ki-pat brought rain to the drought stricken Kapiti Plain.

Rabbit Makes a Monkey Out of Lion: A Swahili Tale. Dial, 1989. With the help of his friend Bush-rat and Turtle, Rabbit makes a fool out of the mighty but slow witted king of the jungle.

Who's in Rabbit's House? Dial, 1977. All of Rabbit's friends except Frog are unsuccessful at getting The Long One out of Rabbit's house.

Why Mosquitos Buzz in People's Ears. Dial, 1975. A cumulative tale that begins with a mosquitos big lie and ends in jungle confusion. Caldecott Award.

Warm-Up Activities

Chant

Swahili Greeting

Divide the children into two groups to do this chant. Each group claps while reciting.

Group One:

Jambo, tembo (JAHM-bow TEM-bow)
[Hello, elephant]

Jambo, rofiki! (JAHM-bow rah-FEE-key)
[Hello, friend]

Group Two:

Jambo, watoto (JAHM-bow wah-TOE-toe)
[Hello, children]

Jambo, rofiki! (JAHM-bow rah-FEE-key)
[Hello, friends]

Repeat with:

chui	(CHOO-e)	leopard
kifaru	(ki-FAH-roo)	rhino
chura	(CHOO-rah)	frog
sungura	(SOON-gu-rah)	hare

Rhyme or Song

Rabbit Lived in Africa (To the tune of "Pop Goes the Weasel")

Rabbit lived in Africa
Along with his friend froggie,
He gets no help from elephant
"Grrrrrr!" says the Long One!

Repeat with jackal, leopard, and rhino.

Follow-Up Activities

Who's in Rabbit's House? Creative Drama
(Starts on page 77)

Use the following script and patterns to present a little creative drama. Enlarge the patterns and trace them on stiff paper or poster board. attach sticks or dowels to the back to make stick puppets. Cover a table with a sheet or tablecloth to create Rabbit's house. Have the child who plays The Long One under the table while reciting his lines. They show themselves at the appropriate time in the script.

Additional Selected Books by Verna Aardema

Misoso: Once Upon a Time Tales from Africa. Knopf, 1994. A collection of twelve folktales from different regions of Africa.

Oh Kojo! How Could You: An Ashanti Tale. Dial, 1984. Relates how a young man named Kojo finally gets the best of the evil trickster Ananse.

Princess Gorilla and a New Kind of Water: A Mpongwe Tale. Dial, 1988. King Gorilla declares that no one shall marry his daughter until he consumes a barrel of strange smelling water.

What's So Funny, Ketu? Dial, 1982. As a reward for saving the life of a harmless snake, Ketu is given the gift of hearing the thoughts of animals.

Who's In Rabbit's House

Adapted by Robin Davis from Who's In Rabbits House by Verna Aardema

Characters:

Narrator 1
Narrator 2
Rabbit
Long One
Frog
Jackal
Leopard
Elephant
Rhino

NARRATOR 1: Long, long ago a rabbit lived on a bluff overlooking a lake. A path went by her door and led down the bank to the water.

NARRATOR 2: All the animals used that path when they wanted to get a drink of water from the lake. Every day, at dusk, Rabbit sat in her doorway and watched the animals. But one evening, something happened...

RABBIT: *Hummm, hummm.* Time to go in my lovely house. *Oh!* What is that noise in my house??

LONG ONE: I am the long One. I eat trees and trample elephants. Go away or I will trample on you!

RABBIT: That's my house. Come out! Come out of my house at once!

LONG ONE: Go away! Or I will trample you!!

(Frog hops up)

FROG: Hello, Rabbit. What is wrong. Why aren't you inside your house eating supper?

RABBIT: Someone is in my house. He won't come out and I can't get in.

FROG: I think I can get him out.

RABBIT: You are too small. Go away! You annoy me! You can't do what I can't do.

JACKAL: Ho, Rabbit. Why aren't you sitting in your house?

RABBIT: Someone is in my house. He won't come out, and he won't let me in.

JACKAL: Yoo, hoo. Who's in rabbit's house?

LONG ONE: I am the Long One and I eat trees and trample elephants. Go away or I will trample you, too.

JACKAL: *Aeiiiiiiii!* I'm going! (Jackal runs off)

RABBIT: Jackal! Please come back! Help me!

(Jackal comes back)

JACKAL: I know what to do. Let's make a big pile of sticks by the door. Next we can set them on fire and burn the Long One out.

RABBIT: Fire! That would burn my house. No, no no! You can't burn my house. Go away!

(Jackal leaves) (Leopard enters)

LEOPARD: Rabbit! Why do you have those sticks by your house? Are you decorating?

RABBIT: No, no, not that. Someone is in my house, and Jackal wanted to burn him out, but it would burn my house, too.

LEOPARD: Yoo hoo, who's in Rabbit's house?

LONG ONE: I am the Long One. I eat trees and trample elephants. Go away or I will trample you, too!

LEOPARD: *Grrrrr!* you don't scare me. I'm tough. I am going to tear that house to bits and eat you up.

RABBIT: Stop, stop, leopard. Don't spoil my house.

LEOPARD: But you can't use it with the long one inside.

RABBIT: But it is still my house! Go away!

(Leopard exits) (Elephant enters)

ELEPHANT: What happened to your house, Rabbit? It has so many scratches.

RABBIT: Someone's in my house, and leopard wanted to tear it to bits and eat him.

ELEPHANT: Yoo hoo! Who's in Rabbit's house?

LONG ONE: I am the Long One. I eat trees and trample on elephants. Go away or I will trample you, too!

ELEPHANT: Trample on elephants? Who thinks he can trample on elephants? I will trample you flat. Flat as a mat. I will trample you, house and all.

RABBIT: No, no elephant, don't smash my house!

ELEPHANT: I'm only trying to help.

RABBIT: I don't want that kind of help. Go away.

(Elephant exits) (Frog laughs)

FROG: Ha ha ha heee heee heee hohoho!

RABBIT: Frog! Are you still here? Stop laughing!

(Rhino enters)

RHINO: Hello, Rabbit, hello Frog. What is so funny??

RABBIT: It is *NOT* funny. Someone is in my house. Elephant wanted to trample him, but she just made big holes in my yard.

RHINO: *Yoo hoo!* Who's in Rabbit's house?

LONG ONE: I am the Long One. I eat trees and trample elephants. Go away or I will trample you, too.

RHINO: Roarrrr! I will hook you on my horn and throw you into the lake - house and all.

RABBIT: No No rhino! Stop, don't toss my house into the lake! *AHHHHHHHHHH!*

(Rhino tosses Rabbit)

RHINO: Well, that's the end of the Long One.

FROG: But you threw RABBIT into the lake!

RHINO: Oh no! Sorry, Rabbit.

RABBIT: Sputter, cough! *OH, BOOOOO HOOOO!* I will never get the Long One out of my house. *Waaaaaaaaa!!!*

FROG: Don't cry Rabbit. I will get the Long One out of your house if you will let me try.

RABBIT: But how?

FROG: Scare him out.

RABBIT: But how??

FROG: Watch me. Yoo hoo, who's in Rabbit's house?

LONG ONE: I am the Long One. I eat trees and trample on elephants. Go away or I will trample you, too.

FROG: *SSSSSSSSSSSS!* Oh no you won't. For I am the spitting Cobra, and I can blind you with my poison. Now come out of Rabbit's house or I will *sssssssss*lither in and spit poison in your eyes.

(Long One is seen for the first time.)

LONG ONE: *AaaaaaaaaaGGGGHHH!* Where's the spitting Cobra? Don't let him spit in my eyes. I was only playing a joke. *HELP!!*

(Long One runs away)

RABBIT: It is only a caterpillar!

FROG: Only a caterpillar! Ha ha ha ha ha!

RABBIT: Oh Long One...Spitting Cobra was only *FROG!*

FROG: Ha ha ha ha ha ha ha!

NARRATOR 1: After that, the animals all went home, except for frog, who sat by Rabbit in her door and laughed all night. If you stay up late, you can still hear Frog laughing.

NARRATOR 1 & 2: *THE END*

Jackal

Elephant

Rabbit

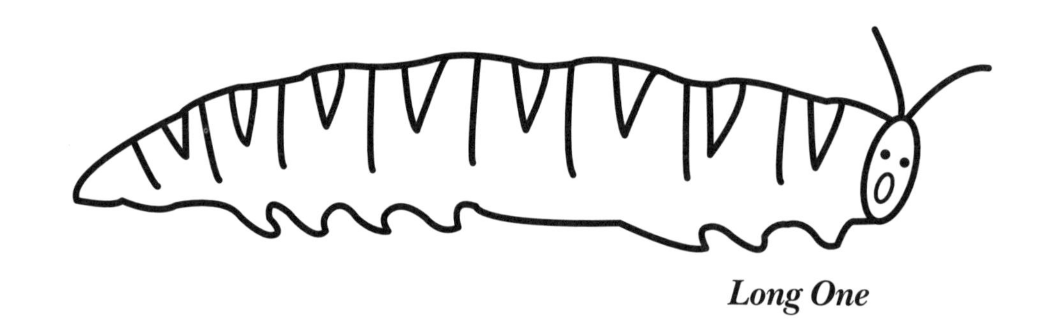
Long One

Frog

Leopard

Rhino

Y *is for ARTHUR YORINKS*

ARTHUR YORINKS has been a writer, teacher, dramatist, mime performer, and script writer for the theater. He has written several plays, many of which have won local awards in New York. He is even making one of his picture books for children, *It Happened in Pinsk*, into an opera.

Born on August 21, 1953 in Roslyn, New York, Yorinks has been involved in the fine arts from a very young age. He took classical piano at age six, and his mother was a fashion illustrator. He liked to draw comic books when he was in high school, and it was then that he first read the picture books of William Steig, Tomi Ungerer, and Maurice Sendak. At age sixteen, he knew that Sendak lived in New York, so he walked right up to his house and asked him to look at some drawings. Mr. Sendak liked the sketches and the artist; they became friends. This was the beginning of Arthur Yorinks career in book illustration.

He is married, and his wife, Adrienne, is a professional dog groomer.

Before Sharing Books

Arthur Yorink's children's books are filled with odd humor generated from strange happenings. Discuss what these happenings are: extraterrestrial visits, transformations, and losing body parts. Ask the children if they find these events humorous, and if so, why? What other strange happenings might they find funny?

Books to Share

Company's Coming. Crown, 1988. Chaos erupts when Moe and Shirley invite some visitors from outer space to stay for dinner with relatives.

Hey, Al! Farrar, Straus and Giroux, 1986. Caldecott Award. The story of Al, a janitor who learns to be thankful for his life as it is.

It Happened in Pinsk. Farrar, Straus, and Giroux, 1987. It is a day in Pinsk that starts out like any other, but becomes unusual for shoe salesman Irv Irving when he discovers something very important missing—his head.

Lois the Fish. Farrar, Straus, and Giroux, 1986. *School Library Journal* Best Book. The story of Louis, a very unhappy butcher who turns into a very happy fish.

Warm-Up Activities

Chant

Funny Birds

Walking in paradise
What do we see?
Strange yellow birds
Laughing at me!

Repeat replacing the word yellow with tall, feathery, etc., and other words derived from the pictures of the birds in Hey, Al!

Action Rhyme

Hey, Al!

If I were a bird, high in the sky,
I'd flap my wings and fly, fly, fly.
(Flap arms)
If I were a dog, I'd go for a run,
And wag my tail, fun, fun, fun.
(Wag body back and forth)
If I were Al, I'd enjoy the day
And I would learn never to say
I'm so unhappy, I'm so blue,
Cause you never know when you might not be you!

Follow-Up Activities

Creative Pantomime

After sharing the book *Hey, Al!*, make your area into a tropical paradise. Tell the children to wear bright clothes, play island music, and serve snacks such as banana slices and coconut. Discuss the story. Was Al happy? What did he do as a job? What does he want? What happens to Al? Next have the children do some pantomime of what Al's transformation was like. What do they think he did when he woke up and found he had a beak and feathers? Pantomime Al and Eddie trying to fly for the first time. What do you think Al did when he found himself back home again?

Additional Selected books by Arthur Yorinks

Bravo, Minski. Farrar, Straus, and Giroux, 1988. *School Library Journal* Best Book. Minski, the greatest scientist who ever lived, invents and discovers everything from electricity to the washing machine. His dream, however, is to sing.

Christmas in July. Harper Collins, 1991. Christmas comes at the wrong time of year after a French dry cleaner misplaces Santa's famous red pants.

Oh, Brother. Farrar, Straus, and Giroux, 1989. *School Library Journal* Best Book. Tells the tale of Milton and Morris, twins orphaned in New York and taken in by a kindly tailor.

Sid and Sol. Farrar, Straus, and Giroux, 1977. Sid, a rather short man, takes on the task of getting rid of the giant, Sol, whose laughs are shaking up the whole world.

Ugh! Farrar, Straus, and Giroux, 1990. Ugh is a small boy made to do all the chores in this prehistoric Cinderella tale.

Z is for *HARVE & MARGOT ZEMACH*

HARVE AND MARGOT ZEMACH were a husband and wife team of children's author/illustrators who created many delightful books until the death of Harve in 1974.

Harve was born in 1933 in New Jersey, and Margot was born in 1931 in Los Angeles. Both were Fulbright Scholars to Austria in 1955; where they met while in Vienna. This talented team adapted and illustrated many folk and traditional tales, including those based on Yiddish stories. Following Harve's death, Margot continued to write and illustrate children's books, creating detailed pen and ink illustrations for her stories.

Before Sharing

Books: Look for classic folklore from around the world at the school or public library. Use Grimm to show examples of Germany, Hans Christian Anderson from Denmark, Joseph Jacobs from England, and Charles Perrault from France. Provide context for each of these tales with a map and some cultural and historical information. Compare these to the folklore written by the Zemachs.

Books to Share

It Could Always Be Worse. Farrar, Straus, and Giroux, 1990. Yiddish folktale of a poor man who gets wise but unusual advice from a Rabbi.

The Judge: An Untrue Tale. Farrar, Straus, and Giroux, 1969. Several people describe the horrible thing that is headed their way, but the judge refuses to believe them.

A Penny a Look. Farrar, Straus, and Giroux, 1971. Two brothers, one rascally and one lazy, and how their get rich plan is turned upon them.

The Princess and the Froggie. Farrar, Straus, and Giroux, 1992. (with Heidi Zemach) Three stories of a princess and her lollipop loving friend, Frog.

Follow-Up Activities

Fairy God Mother

Many of the folktales retold by the Zemachs feature the element of magic. Make your own fairy god mother doll to remember these special books by. Each child will need a 9"x9" cotton or felt square, a fabric marker, a cotton ball, a short ribbon scrap, a pipe cleaner, and a star sticker.

Place the cotton ball in the center of the fabric. Gather the fabric around the cotton ball to form a head. Tie the ribbon around what would be the neck and secure with a bow. Wrap the pipe cleaner around the neck and put the star sticker at the end of one "arm."

Draw a face on the Fairy God Mother using a fabric marker.

Additional Selected Books by Harve and Margot Zemach

Duffy and the Devil. Farrar, Straus, and Giroux, 1986. Duffy, a lazy girl, makes a deal with the devil in a variation of the Rumpelstiltskin tale.

Mommy, Buy Me a China Doll. Farrar, Straus, and Giroux, 1989. A circular folk song about Eliza Lou and her desire for a china doll.

The Three Little Pigs. Farrar, Straus, and Giroux, 1991. Faithfully traditional rendition of the story of three pig brothers and their enemy the wolf.

The Three Wishes. Farrar, Straus, and Giroux, 1980. Three wishes are given to a poor woodcutter and his wife as a reward for rescuing an imp.

Fairy Godmother